Critical Acclaim for

Shortlisted for The Trillium Book Award
Shortlisted for The Stephen Leacock Medal

"[Eliza Clark's] fine first novel ... about a woman's coming of age after the death of her 'soul-mate' mother, has launched her into the literary limelight as one of Canada's most original and quirky fictional voices."

—*NOW Magazine*, Toronto

"A tonic for jaded heartstrings ... Eliza Clark's eye on the world, wacky and true, is a wonder."

—Leon Rooke

"A sweet, ebullient, expansive book ... as hilarious and elastic as a fun-house mirror."

—Susan Dodd

"[*Miss You Like Crazy* is] funny and original ... some beautiful themes are explored, the strongest being the bond that exists, so fragile yet so tough, in the relationship between mother and daughter. Clark's style captures not only the natural flow of speech, but the poetry in reaching for an understanding of life at more than mere face value."

—*The Vancouver Sun*

["Clark] shows an insight into human motivation which few ever develop. She is then able to wrap that up into zany philosophical waxings which can cause a reader to both laugh and cry at the same time."

—*Saskatoon Star-Phoenix*

"First novelist Clark has produced an enormously funny, New Age road saga with unforgettable characters."

—*Library Journal*

"... wild, weird and witty ... beneath the hard laughs the book inspires, there sounds a blues cry for the lost world of simplicity, flowers, and till-death-do-us-part love. At the end ... Maylou seems to have a chance to rediscover that world."

—*The Toronto Star*

"*Miss You Like Crazy* ... introduces a free-spirited, full-steam-ahead talent. Clark spins wild and funny, yet is adept at throwing in tears, memories and hope ... We come away richer, fuller, ready to move on."

—*The Indianapolis News*

"The world Clark creates in this novel is populated with odd characters who speak in strange cliches and curiously poetic language. *Miss You Like Crazy* is a touching yet hilarious and vibrant novel that will be enjoyed."

—*Literature and Language*

Miss You Like Crazy

Miss You Like Crazy

Eliza Clark

HarperPerennial
HarperCollins*Publishers Ltd*

http://www.harpercollins.com/canada

HarperCollins books may be purchased for educational, business, or sales promotional use. For information please write: Special Markets Department, Harper-
Collins Canada, Suite 2900, 55 Avenue Road, Toronto, Canada M5R 3L2.

Canadian Cataloguing in Publication Data
Clark, Eliza
Miss You Like Crazy
ISBN 0-00-648106-X
I. Title
PS8555.L355M5 1999   C813'.54   C98-932569-5
PR9199.3.C42M5 1999

Portions of this novel have been published previously in *The Second Macmillan
Anthology* and *The Malahat Review*.

The author would like to express gratitude to the Canada Council and the
Ontario Arts Council for their support during the writing of this book.
Thanks also to The Banff Centre for the Arts, Leon Rooke, Noel Hudson,
Jennifer Glossop, Steve Baker, Lisa Wray, Michael, and my father, for their time
and encouragement. Published with the assistance of the Ontario Arts Council
and the Canada Council.

For mama in heaven and Michael here beside me.
For Hoodoo his shiny self.

One

MAYLOU WANTED TO FEEL BUOYANT and gung ho. She
wanted to feel like a grand prizewinner in life's sweepstakes,
but with her mama newly dead, buried under ground like a
bulb that could come to pretty flower only in her mind, she
thought herself destined to remain swampy and downtrodden.

The thing about putting on a happy face was trying to
keep it there. A fracas of songs to do with heartbreakage,
living alone, and walking on the sunny side, filled her head.
Maylou pulled "Amazing Grace," sung by Elvis Presley at his
gospel peak, to the forefront of the din. It was the sweetest
sound she knew, self-fortifying, and savage in the most
tender way.

She took a sip of tea. She was seated at a table inside a
storefront window on which a king-size green genie coming
out from a little glass bottle had been painted. Maylou was
one of a handful of people waiting around drinking black-
as-night tea, looking to contact someone dead.

Your Destiny Tea Room had been on East Seventeenth
for nearly forty years and hosted an assortment of psychics,
like Red Dog, Valentine, Sabrina the Gypsy Witch who
once read Priscilla Presley's palm, and Christmas Angel who
worked with the police. Some needed a crystal ball, tarot

cards, well-worn object or palm to read from. Maylou went to Red Dog because of his name and because he needed only tea leaves. The rest was pure ESP.

Maylou's mama had died two months previous after laying down her hand and declaring Gin on her husband, and Doris and Vern Morris, with whom they were playing cards, as usual, in a trailer park in Florida. A triumphant exit. Maylou wanted to bid a fond farewell and maybe catch an earful of truisms. She thought words from her mama might have the gusto to drag her from the torpor she'd sunken into. They might give her the means to be muscular of will, to scold and bristle, and come what may, ditch her love-cheat husband.

Maylou sipped. She ate one of the animal cookies they'd heaped out on a plate. The animals were legless, tailless, headless. She looked around the room. The faces were those of believers. Believers in the power of positive thinking, love that lives on, and the trueness of never say never. Maylou finished her tea and turned the cup facedown on its saucer. She knew she was supposed to make a wish. She turned the cup slowly three times around, hearing china grate on china, thinking, mama mama mama. Just that. Hearing the hard push of china on china, raw and unyielding, the hard push of mother against daughter, daughter against mother, and round again. The cool surface deceptive, belying the bone scarring done with every grinding cycle. Wild as the ache of wishing for a miracle.

Behind a purple curtain, in a room dim and airless, Red Dog reclined. He checked the leaves in Maylou's cup. He pursed his full lips. Old Spice was strong, charmed his nostrils. Maylou sat lightly on the edge of her seat like a petal just fallen to ground.

"What do you see in there?" she said to him.

"M," Red Dog said.

"M for Maylou. Me. I would think."

"Yes, child, but M also for mayhem, metal plate and mama. Initials are less than whole, but more than nothing. Remember that. They are only clues, little more than helpful hints to unseen things. We, in the here-and-now, must do our best to interpret them. We are not magicians, Maylou. Not sorcerers or conjurers or wizards. Is that what you thought, child? I'm sorry to laugh. I know it was innocence on your part."

"Is there anything else in that cup worth mentioning, Red? Did you see the crack on the side, I cut my lip on that, by the way. You should throw it out before harm comes to another." And Maylou ran her tongue across her top lip, pausing at where the split was.

"Not much else. A squirrel with some internal bleeding. Wait," Red Dog said. "A moment." He closed his sixth eye and drifted tranceward. He read her vibes.

"You've had some sadness," he said presently.

"Yes," Maylou said. "You bet I have."

Red Dog's head moved up and down, in a deeper consciousness nod.

"F.A.T. is here," he said in a low-down voice.

"My mama." Her mama's initials, for Florence Anne Turner.

Red Dog's eyelids fluttered. Maylou smiled for her mama.

"Amazing Grace how sweet the sound," Red Dog said. "Hi, Toots," but it was her mama talking, no doubt.

Maylou's eyes filled with tears but she didn't budge them from Red Dog's; she kept looking straight into his eyes, trying to see behind them to where her mama might be.

"Maylou, honey," her mama said, "I have snazzy wings. Imagine me free as a dragonfly, smooth as a pearl. I float around the daytime moon hanging there in your sky like a sideways smile, white against the blue. It's not half bad. If we have love we can never be poor, in the general sense, that is. In life you get what you pay for. Love cannot be bought over the counter with a money-saver coupon. Our love is safe as it could be. Hmm, what else? Everybody has a story to tell. Make a habit of listening with more than your ears. We all want to be happy as clams. Oh, pooh. We've got a bad connection, sweetie, I better go before I get zapped. Hugs and kisses."

Red Dog leaned forward and looked at Maylou as he reached for his cigarettes.

"Okay?" he said.

"Sort of," Maylou said. "It wasn't what I'd hankered after." She stood up unsteadily. Mama, she was thinking, I miss you. Run that by me again. What were you getting at about love and coupons and dragonflies? Maylou wanted to have a conversation. Get things off her chest. Talk like always, back and forth, and come out knowing which way up was. Her mama might have been talking to anybody or their brother, the way it seemed. Maylou wanted to hear things that applied to her situation directly, and illuminated the desirable path like it was the Yellow Brick Road.

"I'm on lunch, sit down awhile if you want," Red Dog said. "Smoke?"

"No," Maylou said, "I can take cigarettes or leave them alone. I'll refrain." But she sat back down. Red Dog lit his and turned it around to watch the end burning.

"When did your mother die?" he asked.

"The beginning of July. In Florida, playing cards, gin rummy, as it turned out."

"Your father was there too. I got a feeling about him. Apart from him being deaf as a rock. He and your mama were in seventh heaven together."

"I guess that they were. Most of the time," Maylou said.

"Something happened when they were married. There was something peculiar that happened," Red Dog said. "Something I can't quite put my finger on."

"It was that my daddy keeled over," Maylou said. "Right after their I do's. In this wrecked-out church they were in. The only things standing were an altar and a life-size Jesus. My mama said that my daddy started swaying like he was drunk, and then his eyes rolled back in his head. Only the whites were there to meet Christ's unshy gaze. He spent out cold turkey. The preacher put his arms around my daddy's waist and dragged him back behind the altar out of sight. My mama said that she could only see the soles of my daddy's new shoes. But she said that they were bright and shiny as a mint dime as they caught and reflected the sunlight coming in through the stained-glass window. My mama said that they were so bright as to be—"

"Heavenly."

"Yes," Maylou said. "So bright as to be heavenly. And she took that as a sign that she hadn't just wedded herself a vegetable. Red?" Maylou took pause. "Were you leading me down the garden path back then? About my mama. Were you bamboozling?"

"No ma'am, I was not. F.A.T. was here."

"Yes," Maylou said. "She was." She knew in her bones it was the real McCoy she'd heard. "It's just there are these things I wanted revealed. Seems I didn't get a word in. A two-way street was not what we were driving down."

"What answers were you seeking?" Red Dog said, drawing on his cigarette like it was the next-best thing.

"Is Emmanuel, my illicit heartthrob, a dream come true?—might be one. Should I take the job at the Beauti-Fuller retail chain or go back and be CeCe's matron of honor? If my life is a pie, how big a slice should I cut for love? Is faith worth the trouble? Who do I talk to now mama's gone? I have a lot of questions, Red."

"Not easy ones either. You should come back. We'll lay out the welcome mat again and hope F.A.T. treads upon it. In the meantime, meditate—you might come up with something on your own. At least we know your mama is a keen spirit, convivial, prompt as an earlybird special."

"I knew she would be," Maylou said. "It's no surprise. She was always coming to my aid. It's just like her to do that. Mama could tell mountains from molehills and which way the wind was blowing. She was a good ally to be in cahoots with. She gave me ample elbow room and was seldom, if ever, crabby."

Maylou thought she'd never once felt alone when her mama was alive. There was a connection they had like twins might, and Maylou trusted it to endure any kind of weather, stormy or fair skies. Nights as a child, before she was ready to go to sleep, Maylou would go into her mama's room and sit in the center of the big, white iron bed, pull the feather comforter over her legs and wait for her mama to get on the bed behind her. She would close her eyes and smell the mingled scents of the clove-studded lemon hung in the closet, rich and spicy, and the faint perfume of the dried flowers her mama scattered on the bottoms of her drawers. Her mama would sit on the bed behind her and brush Maylou's long, black hair a hundred strokes until it was like fine velvet and hung in shining glory down her back. While she brushed, her mama would count the strokes softly under her breath, and Maylou would let her mind go blank and feel the tug of the brush on her scalp and the rhythmic glide down past her shoulders, hard and gentle, both. Neither spoke until the hundred count had been reached and the hairbrush with the real silver handle put away on the dresser. Then Maylou and her mama would lie down together on the old bed and talk about the day, or whatever it was came into their minds. Often they fell asleep that way, side by side like girlfriends, or chaste sweethearts, and Maylou's father would have to spend the night sleeping in Maylou's single bed. Not once did he complain, though, or dare come between them, maybe recognizing that he was on the outside of something special and would never have been allowed close to it anyway. Maylou knew her mama's love. She knew it ran through her mama's veins just the same as the blood did, and the oxygen. Straight through her heart.

"I hear longing, unfettered grief behind your words," Red Dog said, eyeing Maylou through his tobacco fog. "What are you after, child?"

"I want to foxtrot, tango and samba. I want to be light on my feet and go waltzing around. I want to pull an ace from my sleeve and have a full house. I want to dance the last dance cheek-to-cheek with my mama," Maylou said, blazing some passion.

"But the gig's up," Red Dog said. "There's no getting milk when the cup is empty. I see dearly beloveds willing to give their eyeteeth for another shot at it. One more kiss, one more word, one more something, to set the record straight once and for all. Love is shy, but most of us know when we're being winked at. We know love like we know the backs of our hands. Your mama was attuned to the melody of your heartstrings, rest assured. You can't keep dancing, child, when the music has stopped."

"But, Red, the band plays on," Maylou said. "Listen. I hear the sound of harp and flute, the distant fluttering of a new angel. I hear the gentle tapping of a perfect foot."

Two

THE ESP PARTY-LINE COMMUNICADO piqued Maylou to the cemetery where her mama was laid to rest. Driving through the black iron gates, there were grounds on either side, and a long and winding road that spanned the length from front to back. Emmanuel, whose eyes Maylou admired for being the exact color of antifreeze, had his van parked on the shoulder with the side doors open to display buckets of fresh cut flowers. Emmanuel's heart itself was as rosy as any wild field flower, with petals that queried daily "she loves me, she loves me not" for Maylou.

Topeka's Gates of Heaven cemetery was the kind that allowed no standing monuments. Instead, square bronze ground plaques, with attached vases that pulled up for flowers or laid flat for when there weren't any, covered the rolling hills as far as could be seen.

Maylou knew exactly where her mama was. Not like the first time. The first time she came with her husband, Zak, and his sister Tilly, and they couldn't find the grave. They initially were looking all together, Maylou calm. Then they split up, and Maylou saw Zak stooped over plaques far to her right and Tilly walking lightly, looking to her left. Tilly was very beautiful, with a face like a sweet moon and eyes blue as Zak's, but deeper. Maylou was reading names—Matthews, Zimmerman, Hughes. But no F.A.T. Where was her mama? In which row of dead people lay her mama? It seemed the cemetery went on forever, and there was Maylou standing small as a pea with her flowers for her dead mama who died playing cards, and Zak and Tilly now far away as they walked studying the ground. From deep in her stomach came a cry so loud that Maylou felt it rising before she heard its sound. So loud it became that it shattered her heart to pieces. And Maylou fell to the ground after her broken heart. Tilly heard the wail, stopped and turned, and came running over. She fell to the earth on Maylou and rocked her, pressing her moonface into Maylou's hair. Then Zak was calling that he'd found it. And Maylou and Tilly got up and walked slowly over to where Zak was. There were already flowers in the vase, pale daisies from Maylou's father, John. And Maylou looked down on all that was left of her mama.

A bronze plaque with her name, the day she was born and the day that she died playing cards, a rose, and an intertwined knot below which was written "Together Forever"; one half of the knot would be Maylou's father when he died. John loved Flossie more than anything else, maybe more than she'd loved him. But Flossie for sure had loved her daughter more than life itself. She had tried for twenty-one years to conceive her, so when after three miscarriages the rabbit finally died again, she stayed in bed the whole of her pregnancy with Maylou, so that no bump of a car or mean look would jostle this baby out. When it came time to deliver, Flossie had become so attached to the baby that the umbilical cord formed a noose around Maylou's neck, preferring to strangle her own child than to let it slip out and away. When Maylou was freed at last from her forty-two-year-old mama, they clung tight. Understanding that pearly bond between the top and bottom shells of a clam.

Thunder clouds swung low over the cemetery's wrought-iron gates. Since rain was on its way, Maylou got out her manicure scissors. Trimming the grass around the tombstone was something she found both useful and soothing. First she'd brush away the clippings left from the mowers, then she'd take her manicure scissors and cut back the grass that grew out over her mama's name and the love-knot relief.

Looking at Maylou from a distance, a passerby or another mourner might think she was younger than mid-twenties, maybe twelve or fourteen. She was thin, with coal dark hair that hung straight down her back as it had for as long as she could remember. She wore layers of flowered skirts one over the other in a leggy bouquet and seemed part gypsy, part flower child, part waif. She looked to be filled with secrets. In her dreams only was everything black and white.

While she prettied the ground, Maylou thought about her mama dying. Playing cards like that. Gin and then boom, cashed in her chips for wings. And Doris Morris cleaning out her mama's closet right after, saying that her mama had a lot of nice things she herself could put to good use while she was still living. Taking everything, even the Tender Tootsies that smelled of too many flea market haunts under the hot Florida sun.

The rain began. Maylou packed away her scissors, and saw Emmanuel coming her way with an umbrella. He looked like Heathcliff.

"Here, babe," he said, handing her the umbrella. He crouched down beside her. "You haven't been around so much," he said as he stroked her hair.

"No, not as much as before." Maylou turned to look right into his turquoise eyes. She couldn't stand it and looked away.

"Maylou," he said as he put his hand under her chin to raise her head. "Maylou, don't you want to see me? I've missed you. She pulled her head away. "Maylou," Emmanuel said.

"I've missed you," she said. "It's just I've had things needed doing." She glanced at him, he seemed hurt.

"Maylou, when are you going to marry me?" he said full steam, but quiet.

"I'm married to Zak," Maylou said meeting his eyes. "I'm married for better or worse, supposably."

"To Zak. He ain't worth the shoes he stands in."

Maylou thought that might be true.

"I can't. Even if Zak's not Mr. Right for me."

"Why not? Why can't you?"

Maylou was pricking her thigh with the manicure scissors in her pocket. "Because you've never said you love me, because I hardly know you. Time needs to go by."

"You know I love you," Emmanuel said and turned his eyes on her. He held her face in both his hands. "I love you," he said, "like a rock." And it was so true it rang out. She had no doubt. She fingered the "together forever" on her mama's grave. She touched his cheek with the stubble on it and the rain.

"You love me," he said. "You love me too."

Maylou buried her face in his coat. She knew that she did. They stayed there for some time, a monument, alone in the cemetery. Then Emmanuel helped her up and they walked back to his van.

The van was hard to miss because it was psychedelic, all pink and purple and orange, flowers and swirls, and said FLOWER POWER on the side. Emmanuel had bought it cheap from a group of hippie-gypsies, as he called them, who were looking to sell it after one of their band members had fallen off the rocking chair they'd strapped to the roof.

Earl, the bearded and beaded man, had slid down the front windshield, still rocking, before finally slipping underneath the van's front tires. Emmanuel loved bright colors, and told how when he'd noticed the van while paying homage to a dead cousin, he couldn't resist going over to it for a closer look. It was rusted in spots, and he was chipping at the rust a little with his fingernail when one of the hippies had come over to him. Levon, who owned the van, was a cross between a Temptations band member and a Hell's Angel. He'd bent to see what Emmanuel was doing.

"Hey, don't touch the merchandise, man," Levon had said, swiping at where Emmanuel was picking.

"It's a great van," Emmanuel had said. "A real treasure trove."

"It's a death mobile," Levon had answered. "A vehicle of deliverance," he'd sighed and paused heavily, "to the beyond."

"That's cool," Emmanuel had said, trying to be hip.

"Cool? What planet are you from?" Levon had looked down on Emmanuel's plain shoes.

Emmanuel, in return, had looked at Levon's striped socks sticking out from his sandals, and upped his eyebrow. "Earth," he'd said. "But I dig your van. Very much."

"A hundred and fifty, dude, and it's your bronco to bust."

"Cool then," Emmanuel had said, counting bills into Levon's curly palm.

Emmanuel had climbed behind the wheel and revved the engine while he watched Levon and the other hippies walking across the cemetery grounds towards the heavy iron gates. Some of the women had danced as they went, their hair flying out behind them like firesparks. It was then that Emmanuel had put two and two together. Flower Power plus cemetery. He would use his van to sell flowers from. His market research was lying beneath the ground all around him. He would be self-employed. He'd smiled to himself, and revved his freedom.

Maylou was lounging next to Emmanuel on the love seat he'd fixed into the van for them almost two months earlier. They'd begun their adulterous entanglement by passing pleasantries on Maylou's visits to her mama's grave. Some had led to more, and then to out-and-out hanky-panky of a honeyed and tender ilk. Now Emmanuel wanted to know which the last petal on the stalk was going to be.

"Maylou, let me get to know you. Let me make it right. If your man's gone salty on you, give me a try," he said.

"Emmanuel, I'm a bad bone through and through," she said. "I could give you a lasting complex."

He pulled her tight. "If you're a bad bone, I'm a monkey's uncle," he said.

Maybe he was, Maylou thought, a monkey's uncle, and she smiled sweetly at him.

"Okay, I'll tell you about me," he said, "then we'll be on the track to knowing each other. We never had any money when I was a kid. The only thing I had to play with was a hot water bottle with a little sweater on it. Later I got a kitten, but it drowned in the toilet. I put the body, dripping, into a shoebox in the back of my closet. My mama found it there a few weeks later and gave me royal hell for putting it in the same box with my church shoes, which I hadn't thought to take out." Emmanuel looked at Maylou. "I didn't go to church all that often."

She moved closer to him. "Why not?"

"Why not?" he said. "Well, because my shoes were ruined."

"No really," Maylou said, "be square."

"Well, I had this aunt. Not a real aunt, she took care of us."

"Who's us?"

"My brother and I. She was a soloist in the church choir. She had the voice of an angel. She would shout the church, get everybody going, me too, swaying and singing with our arms reaching up to Him, to the Light. And this one time she was singing and doing her thing, moving her hips back and forth in her shining white dress that let all her womanhood show through, and she made a man die of heart failure right then and there in the church. And his wife screamed as he slumped onto her, but we all thought he was reeling in the Glory. And the Amens went up. And the Hosannas too. Then when the music stopped, we found out he was dead. And Aunt Lucille stopped singing for good right then. She said that her songbird had flown away, leaving only birdseed in its place."

"Oh, that's sad," Maylou said.

"I guess it is," Emmanuel said. "He probably had heart rot to start with, nothing to do with my Aunt Lucille. That's what's sad about it."

"Heart rot?" Maylou said.

"A hereditary kind of thing. What happened with your own mama, sugar?" he said. "Tell me so we'll know each other."

Maylou looked into the crystal sea of his eyes. "I love you," she said all sudden. "I just do." And Zak, her legally wed man, faded to gray.

"I love you," Emmanuel said. "Ditto, I do." Then a customer came and bought some hollyhocks. The rain beat down on the van. Emmanuel came back wet, with a flower head in his hand for her. He put the flower through her buttonhole.

"Delta Dawn, what's that flower you have on?" he said.

"Could it be a faded rose," Maylou answered.

"From days gone by." He kissed her.

Emmanuel took Maylou's hand in his palm. It was pale and thin, with long fingers tipped by perfect flush ovals. He closed his own brown fingers around it, and Maylou saw him looking at the scratches and scars he had jagging his hands from the rough stems he had to deal with every day. There was a thorn still lying under the surface of the skin on one of his fingers and once he saw it, Maylou imagined he might feel it too, pricking him ceaselessly, though not enough to draw blood.

"You know part of it already. I just can't sum up and tell you the whole thing," Maylou said. "My mama died in Florida and my daddy and I brought her back in an urn. In the back of the station wagon. With CeCe too, Bubba's wife. At night I didn't know whether or not to bring my mama into the motel or leave her out with the luggage." Maylou turned to him. "What would you have done, if you were me?"

Emmanuel thought. "I guess I might have brought her in at night. Into the hotel."

"That's what I did." Maylou leaned her head against her new man's shoulder. She found this talk about her mama wearying. Explaining was hard since she didn't know what order to put everything in. The real order felt as random to her as though the events had been tossed up and scattered like chicken feed.

Emmanuel laid his head crowning Maylou's.

"I yearn to hitch myself to you," he said, "no holds barred. Stay by me, sugar, and we'll live in clover. You'll never want."

"But I do want," Maylou said. And with that she plucked the hollyhock from her buttonhole and put it in her mouth. She chewed it carefully and smiled up at Emmanuel, the flower spread lovely across her bared teeth.

Three

MAYLOU'S MOTHER WAS DEAD, lying in the hospital at Largo. Maylou had been to Largo once and could imagine the palm trees swaying in the warm breeze outside the hospital, no doubt a square gray building tastefully landscaped outside, and carefully decorated inside, to provide a sense of peaceful seclusion for the sick and tired. Everything would be cast a rosy pink like the underbelly of a shell. It was something about the southern light. It would make a nice place to pass away in. Maylou's father had said that her mother looked just like she'd been sleeping, tanned and healthy. He said that he'd waited at first, expecting her to open her eyes as soon as the doctors left the room. When she hadn't, he'd waited longer. Then he'd held and kissed her hand and slowly removed her wedding ring. He'd slid the band down onto his own finger and it had gone easily into place. Their hands, his wife's and his, had always been the same size, they'd compared them pressed like living fossils into wet sand. He'd never worn a wedding ring. Men didn't when he was married, especially if they used their hands in their work. But he wanted to wear one now. Until he was the one lying dead and even then he thought he'd like to be buried wearing it.

Maylou searched through the phonebook for the number of the airline she needed to book her flight to Florida. As she ran her finger down the page, she thought of all the people the names belonged to. Most of them would be alive, sitting at home in front of the TV watching Oprah Winfrey and drinking Martini & Rossi sweet vermouth over ice. Some of them would be dead though, she figured. They'd have to be. C. Amendola might be dead. She could call the number beside his name and find out, but it wouldn't be right to do that. Hi, may I speak to C. Amendola or is he dead already? People die all the time. But not your mother. Your mother only dies once, and usually her name's not listed in the phonebook to begin with.

Maylou sat on the plane to Florida next to Renee Louisianna Harp, a fattie with a heart of gold. Renee Louisianna had done herself up for the plane ride and kept rearranging to show to her best advantage. She was wearing a silky rayon blouse with a tropical fruit theme patterned on it. In no time at all she had pulled out snapshots of her only son, Pernell, a big-headed boy with bright eyes and a side part lying almost on top of his left ear.

"This here's Pernell eating a sloppy Joe," she said. Maylou took the dog-eared photograph and studied it for a minute before passing it back.

"Pernell can sometimes eat three of those at a sitting, if you can believe that, with two cream puffs for dessert afterwards. That's when he's feeling like himself. He's still in mourning at the present time, though." Renee L. was fishing through her handbag for some talc, which she found and sprinkled generously on her wrists and palms.

"Sweaty palms," she said, "like my mother and my grandmother before me. You know what they say, 'cold hands, warm heart,' but they never say anything about hot hands. Lord knows I'm not coldhearted if that follows, not in the least. Unless I'm provoked. When I'm provoked I change my colors altogether, like a chameleon. You wouldn't even know it was me you were looking at."

"Why is Pernell in mourning?" Maylou asked, thinking maybe they had something in common, she and the boy.

"Oh, it's sad, that story. Pernell's daddy got him this baby cockatiel for his birthday, 'cause Pernell had been going on and on about getting a bird and how he'd look after it and all, and so we thought it might be a good idea. Teach him some responsibility for another living creature. But this bird was crippled with a busted foot. It had its foot twisted almost right around on itself, and Pernell took it to the vet and the vet broke the foot and set it back the way it should've been from the start. It had a dressing of white gauze wrapped around and around its tiny ankle that Pernell had to change every morning. Well we, Basil my husband, and I, thought it was important to leave Pernell alone to do the doctoring, we made sure he had enough gauze and all, but we let him be. Anyway a week goes by, and I happen to be in Pernell's room making up his bed when he's changing the dressing. And I smell this horrible smell. It was like ... " Renee searched.

"Rotten eggs," Maylou offered.

"Yeah," said Renee L., nodding slowly, "but worse, kind of like ... " Maylou waited, trying to think of something else, some worse smell. "Like a chili fart," Renee Louisianna said, and paused to let the full horror of that particular smell come to Maylou's memory.

"And I dropped the bedsheet and went and looked at that poor bird's crippled foot. Well I can't tell you how swollen

and puffed it was, blue and yellow and inflamed. I almost
screamed, the poor sad little creature. I whacked Pernell
good; I don't know what he could have been thinking of.
But I guess he honestly didn't know any better. He'd never
seen infection before. So I wrapped the foot up loosely and
put the bird, Birdy he was called, in the back seat, and Pernell
rode up front with me, to the vet's. But here's where the
tragedy comes. On the way there, Birdy chewed off his own
sore foot, and when Pernell turned around, there was Birdy
still pecking at the bloody stump, and the infected foot lying
clear across on the other side of the cage where he'd pitched
it. Pernell was scarred for life. He choked and started pulling
at my arm while I was driving till I thought for sure we'd run
off into the ditch. I had no idea what had happened. Who
would've thought that Birdy would maim himself in such a
brutal way? But then I guess that's nature in the raw, taking
care of itself. It was something that Pernell had to learn the
hard way, I guess." Renee L. was shaking her head and trying
to pry off her high-heeled pumps with the toe of one put to
the heel of the other, but due to the air pressure her feet had
swollen and the shoes could only be pulled off by hand.

"Honey, I hate to bother you this way, but my shoes just
won't come unstuck, would you reach down there and ... "

"Surely," Maylou said, and undid her safety belt and
pulled off the shiny black pumps, half expecting the fat feet
to come off in them.

"So what happened to that bird, Birdy? Did it die on the
way to the vet's after all?" Maylou asked, drying off her palms
discreetly, sticky from the wet nylons.

"No ma'am, it did not die. In fact the vet said it was the
best thing that could of happened. Here take this," Renee
L. said, handing Maylou a Kleenex. "No, Birdy still hops
around on one foot, you hear it at night on the bottom of

the tin cage. Tap, tap, tap. Tap, tap, tap." Renee L. used her index finger to charade the one-legged bird hopping.

"So why is Pernell in mourning then if his bird didn't die?" Maylou thought maybe the point had flown past her along the way.

"We're not sure exactly why. We think maybe he's just mourning after what might have been. A perfect world where all birds have enough feet. You know kids, they get these notions."

Just then the stewardess brought them their in-flight meal of filet mignon wrapped in bacon, with carrots and mashed potatoes. There was also a coleslaw salad, a jelly roll for dessert, and a cup for tea or coffee. Renee Louisianna took a good look at her portion of meat, which she got first, then at Maylou's, but since Maylou's filet looked smaller, substantially smaller, Renee L. seemed satisfied.

"I'm ready for this," she said, tucking in. "That'll be Kentucky bluegrass down there," she said, waving a fork over Maylou as she looked out the window. Maylou had the window seat but since they were seated directly on the wing, there was nothing to see anyway. Unless the plane tilted on a real angle, which made Maylou so nervous that she wouldn't look out.

"You know it's green, not blue, that grass. My Lord, I'm feeling like particular hell today," Renee Harp said. "Look at my complexion all pasty and bumped," she rubbed her fingertips across her cheek and stuck out her chin. Maylou looked, but didn't notice too much wrong with Renee L.'s face, except for the roll of fat making another chin under the primary one. "Did you know that ninety percent or so of household dust is skin? Just dead skin that's fallen off and covers the top of the TV and the lampshades. I didn't know that until quite recently when I read it somewhere. It changes the way you look at things, knowing that. It makes you wonder what else, what other things you don't know about. Day-to-day things you should have some information on. Renee L. took a huge forkful of coleslaw then, some of which fell off into her lap and made her laugh a bit in shame.

"First thing I'm going to do is settle myself into a roomette in Tampa–St. Pete," she went on. "I'm going to strip down and lie naked on the bed and let the air-conditioning make me shiver. I might sleep that way for an hour or so."

Maylou was picking at her jelly roll when the plane lurched in such a manner as to make her tray slide across in front of Renee L., who stopped it by putting a finger on the jelly roll and pushing it back to her that way. Maylou was wearing her hair back in a long braid, and she guessed by the way she was now being examined she didn't look all that spunky.

"Where are you off to, I never did ask," Renee L. said, honing in on the dark circles under Maylou's bleary eyes. "I can be so preoccupied with my own self I don't notice anyone else's put a vacancy sign up in the window needs some attending to."

"Largo," Maylou said. "My mama just died there and I've got to drive my father back home and take care of things."

"Um-hm, like the cremation and all. Florida State law. I know all about it. I had to have my Uncle Castor done not even a year ago this coming Christmas. Let me just advise you one thing, if I may—don't feel like you've got to spend a lot of money on the urn for your dear mama's ashes. Only a fool is money proud. Remember that. Those urns are more costly than you'd think. My Lord, are they ever. Just choose wisely, your mama will understand. What happened to her anyway?"

"She was playing cards and they thought she was laughing because she'd won, but she wasn't: she was gasping for breath. Her heart gave out on her."

"Kaput," Renee Harp said sympathetically, shaking her head. "Too much excitement, I suppose. Who was she playing against?"

"My father. And Doris and Vern Morris." Maylou could feel herself tightening.

"Doris Morris? Good God, what the hell kind of name is that for a human being."

"I don't know, I never met her. They're going to drive my father to the airport to meet me. I guess you'll see her then too."

"I'll keep my eye out, I'd hate to miss that one." And then Renee Louisianna settled back to nap and Maylou got back to the book she was reading called *The Elvis Murders*.

Maylou had always read. She was inspired by her nanna who loved reading and storytelling as much as she loved Lawrence Welk. Maylou used to sit on her lap and listen to stories that her nanna had made up herself from scratch and others that she'd added to, to suit Maylou's special tastes. *Beauty and the Beast* was Maylou's favorite, the Beast being a kind of kangaroo with teeth like a piranha. Maylou always had a thing about teeth, and she liked the idea of being hopped around in a kangaroo's pouch. Most of the time the stories ended badly, with Maylou as Beauty being chewed and left scarred or limbless to hobble off behind a white rose bush and pine away. Maylou liked this better, preferred it to a rosy-hued Harlequin ending, as did her nanna herself, if the truth be known. Maylou's nanna spent her last years in a nursing home, and died while having her hair done by the in-house hairdresser at the Golden Age Coiffure Hut they had set up on the main floor. You could tell when it was she died, because there was one section of hair at the nape of her neck that was straight as a pin, where the hairdresser hadn't bothered to finish.

Getting off the plane, the heat hit like an oven door being opened. Renee L. carried a large over-the-shoulder bag and a straw hat, and there was already perspiration across her top lip. Maylou was feeling apprehensive about seeing her father and the unknown Morrises, Doris and Vern. Though she did hope Oscar would be there. Oscar was her wiener dog of seventeen years. Just after Maylou married Zak, Oscar had packed up camp and hit the dusty trail. He'd sensed a certain disdain coming from Zak that had made the hairs on the back of his neck bristle. So one day when Maylou's father was over, Oscar had seized the moment and followed him into his car and wouldn't come out again, even for a plate of cold beans. Maylou could understand it in a way. Her choice of Zak didn't necessarily have to suit anyone else, but still she missed Oscar and the fun they'd had.

"God, it's hotter than hell, isn't it, Maylou?" Renee Louisianna said, fanning herself with her hat as they waited for their bags to come.

"I don't guess that it is, after all," Maylou said, thinking that fatties always sweat more and feel hotter.

"I guess you're right, sweetie pie, I'm always stretching the truth like an elastic band. If I wasn't so fat I'd be cool as a cucumber now, I bet," Renee L. said.

"You're not fat," Maylou said, falsely and soft.

"No, you're right, honey bunch," Renee stepped in. "I'm not fat, I'm just fluffy." And she got a good laugh at her old joke. Maylou had this image of the rhyming woman, Doris Morris, waiting for her behind the barrier, and couldn't laugh herself.

Once through the gates Renee Louisianna gave Maylou a big hug and pinched her arm.

"You take care now, sugar loaf," she said. "I took the liberty of scribbling my sister's phone number on the back cover of that Elvis book you were reading. She'll know how to get hold of me when you want. Call me up and we'll have a heart-to-heart sometime soon. I feel like we're already that close."

And as she walked away, Maylou checked the back jacket of her book and there it was—Renee Louisianna Harp c/o Carolina Rosetta Harp (her Sister) (813) 499-2376 Call Me!!— all in this flowery print, except for the exclamation marks at the end, which were threats, reinforced with double lines. Maylou carefully tore off the back jacket of her book and ripped it in half. She meant to throw both halves into a nearby garbage container, but she missed, and only one half made it into the can, the other half fell onto the floor behind it. That half read: (813) 499-2376 Call Me!!

Maylou imagined a lonely janitor finding the message while cleaning later that night and calling the number that appeared so anxious to be called. Not long after, she thought, he might end up marrying the fattie sister spinster, Carolina Rosetta Harp. Maylou left the note on the floor towards this purpose, hoping the janitor might live happily ever after, thanks to her and what he would term Precious Fate, with heart-sworn reverence.

Four

DORIS MORRIS STOOD THERE LIKE DIRT, and Vern beside her. He looked like some kind of has-been or never-was country singer, all faded and loose and stepped on. She had an Orange Julius in her hand and a red mole on her forehead off to the right, that seemed it would deflate her head like a beach ball if you pulled at it. She was common, with the kind of bad posture that comes from years of being wrong. She wasn't at all fat, tender mercy. Not at all.

Maylou's father wore the yellow cardigan Maylou had given him as a present and looked like a pulled tooth, and the gaping sore hole from a pulled tooth, at the same time. His pain spun round his face and his head like a halo edging upwards to heaven. Glowing and glorious, needy and right-ful. Maylou thought of small fragile things—fingers, teardrops and pins. She was hurting. And she was mad. Doris Morris could take her skinny bones elsewhere in a hurry.

"Daddy," Maylou said and buried herself and swallowed him up. This made him cry and her cry in front of Doris Morris regardless. Vern took her bag and they walked through the airport to where Vern's car was. John held Maylou against him as they walked, and she knew things would never be the same. Her mama gone.

"Your mama was my best friend, honey, I want you to know, even though it was just on two months that we knew each other, all totalled. You know how that is sometimes. Like sisters. We hit it off from scratch and unravelled our secrets like they were true confessions. Things about you too. You'd be surprised by our closeness. Maybe this isn't the time, but you know what her last word was? You should probably know what it was." Doris waited. So did Maylou. "To remember for always," Doris said.

Thoughts crossed Maylou's mind—tell Maylou to take good care. Tell my sweetest Maylou to mind her p's and q's. Tell Maylou I'll miss her. Or maybe more likely, just "Maylou," her only daughter's name, said as only a dying mama can say it. Whispered as she faded, as she met her maker and floated above her body, that earthly thing she'd discarded for laundry.

"Doris," Doris said. "That was her last word. Doris." And Doris looked to her husband for confirmation.

But meek and drawlingly, Vern said, "I take pride I'm an honest man. In truth I didn't hear that at all, not my wife's name spoken in any way at all."

Doris rolled her eyes, spurned him. "You sure are honest," she said. "Honest as the day is long. And it's so long and so honest, Vern, it's completely boring. You and your pickypicky attitude have made you blind. Blind to a lot of the world's simple pleasures, and kindly deceptions." Doris pinched Vern a little and he pulled his arm away.

She nodded at Maylou. "Anyway, it is a true fact, that's what your mama said. And then I held her hand till the ambulance came, didn't I, Vern? You've got to give it to them, they got there quick. Couldn't have been more than five, less even, maybe three, three and a half minutes. What do you think, Vern, it was maybe three minutes till they came?" She looked to Vern, ready to pinch.

"Maybe a tad longer. But not much I guess," he said. "They was there fast." He appeared relieved to have an honest answer he could give. He felt better about his wife, Maylou could tell, going by the way he would have stroked her arm if she hadn't pulled it away like a lightning bolt.

"These last thirty-six hours have been terrible," Doris said. "I'm all on edge like a cat on hot tin. My calm pills are nowhere in visible sight, of course."

Vern slung Maylou's bag into the trunk with some effort, though it wasn't heavy, since Maylou figured she'd just wear the same things over again and hadn't packed much. It was the notions weighed it down, she would've bought travel sizes if she'd had extra time. She squeezed her daddy's hand.

"It'll be all right," she said as they got into the back seat. Looking at the rear of Doris Morris's head offered some relief. Better than looking at the front. But not much.

The Florida night air was humid and soft, and it was good to have the windows down. John had his face pressed to the air with his eyes shut, still crying on their own. Maylou had vowed to herself to keep holding onto his hand until they got out of the car, when she'd have to let go. The blood in her hand was his blood, and her mama's blood, and her own blood mixed, like a family transfusion. The power in that was a kind of gospel song she could hear floating up between their fingers, giving her strength. It was important not to let go.

On the dash was a turkey claw. Not unfresh-looking, cut off at the ankle.

"What's the turkey claw for?" Maylou asked.

Doris turned from the window and picked it up.

"Luck. A turkey foot for luck," she said. "I try and always keep me a fresh turkey foot on the dash for luck. It's just something I've always done. Isn't it, Vern?"

But Maylou could tell Vern remembered a time when Doris hadn't put a turkey foot on the dash because he didn't answer, and he looked down at the untruth, the discrepancy between fact and fiction. Doris sighed.

"See, the tendon is still intact," she said. And she reached into the foot slightly and pulled what looked like a string. The claw clenched. She opened and closed it, pulling the string. Then she put it back on the dash gently.

"Where do you get them?" Maylou asked.

"Here and there," Doris said. "They're not hard to come by if you know where to look."

"The A & P'll usually give 'em to you if you ask," Vern said and looked to Doris to confirm. She was gazing out the window again. "Won't they give 'em to you at the A&P?" Vern repeated. Doris turned and stared at him. She sighed again.

"They will," she said, "but they're not always as fresh there as other places. Give it a rest, Vern."

Vern tapped the turkey foot. "We've had pretty good luck all in all since we've been putting these things on the dash. Except for your mama dying with us playing cards, and that car wreck our boy was in. But that could've been worse. I'd have to say they work. They do bring luck." Maylou smiled at him in the rearview. He was just looking away when he caught her smiling. It had been a long time since anyone had smiled directly at him. He grinned like a madman. Doris saw and sighed.

"Vern, watch your speed," she said.

They drove past oak trees hung with Spanish moss, and palmettos and cypress. Doris wore a sorry face most of the way, but seemed to brighten as they entered the gates of the trailer park and saw Bubba out front in the blackberry patch. There was a little Negro girl beside him with a straw hat on, holding Oscar who was trying to get away. Poor Oscar, Maylou thought, what an unsavory life he's had so far, for a wiener dog. Spying Doris, the little girl dropped him and fled.

"Bubba," Doris called, "this here's Maylou come to see after Flossie. Go and fetch that snack plate I made up." She turned to Maylou. "Just a little something to tide you over," she said. "Potato salad and chicken sandwiches. And some taco chips."

Vern pulled into the driveway of a trailer Maylou had seen pictures of. It was painted periwinkle blue and had hazelnut and chokecherry bushes lining the walkway up to it. There were two window boxes painted white, holding some hanging pink flowers. It was pretty in its own way. You could tell care had been given to transform it from a trailer into a home. John looked at it sadly. Maylou squeezed his hand, then let go.

They got out of the car just as Bubba bolted into the trailer next door. Its yard was littered with children's toys and overturned potted plants and bits of wood. Bubba came out with a tray in his hands covered with plastic wrap that he was carrying too carefully for what was on it. Vern got Maylou's bag out of the trunk and made a big deal of carrying it inside for her. Nothing was too much since the smile. John went in, then Vern, then Bubba. Doris pointed to the dumpy trailer next door and told Maylou that was where she lived, with the extended family. The woman standing in the doorway holding the kid was CeCe, Bubba's wife. The kid was Lawrence, he was four. Oscar was there too now, sitting on the front step watching Maylou tiredly. They made a sight, the three of them watching her. She turned to go into her daddy's pretty trailer home and Doris Morris followed behind.

Inside, the men were sitting like stones around the kitchen table. Bubba was scratching his arm, and Maylou saw that he had a spiderweb tattoo that stretched halfway up to his shoulder and halfway down to his wrist. The apex was a large black spider sitting right on his elbow. Bubba caught Maylou looking and flexed a little, making a breeze go through the web.

"This here's my only son Bubba," Doris said. "Bubba meet Maylou, she's Flossie's only girl. See we have, we had, so much in common." Doris sniffed and Bubba got up to care for his mama and pulled out a chair. Doris sat and looked at her snack plate sitting on the table. The wrap was still on it and she peeled it back.

"What happened to the taco chips?" she said. They all looked at the plate, even John, who had been staring down at the table in front of him.

"I guess it was CeCe," Bubba said. "I heard her crunching in the other room, but I didn't know it was the taco chips she was eating. I had no idea that's what it was."

"I explained to her what the snack plate was for," Doris said with an edge. "You'd think it was CeCe, not you, who had a steel plate in their head."

"Mama," Bubba said looking sheepishly at Maylou. They sat in silence then. They were waiting on Maylou and she knew it.

"I guess I'll make some coffee," she said. "Would you all like some? Daddy, can I make some coffee for you?"

"Yes, I'll have some coffee," John said, reaching out his hand for Maylou to hold. "What are we going to do without your mama? I don't know," he said, shaking his head. "I don't know what we're going to do. I'm all on my own."

Doris hopped up then and went behind him and put her arms around his neck. "He's been this way ever since," she said to Maylou. "The poor thing, lost his ladylove. They were such a nice couple, lovebirds in every way." John began to cry.

Maylou went into her bag for the canned black cherries she'd brought with her. She put the can on the kitchen counter and started hunting for an opener.

"What's that?" Doris said.

"Black cherries," Maylou said, opening the can.

"You brought a can of black cherries with you on the plane?" Doris said.

Maylou stopped and turned. "I also brought some salt-water taffy and pecan rolls," she said eyeing Doris, the can opener in her hand.

"I'll have some of that saltwater taffy, if it's available," Bubba said. Maylou shifted her gaze to him.

"It's in my bag," she said.

Bubba came back with the taffy. "How much did they stick you for this?"

"Eighty-nine cents," Maylou said thinly.

"Eighty-nine cents? They must've seen you coming," he said. "That's for sure. You can get it cheaper just about anywhere around here. Just about anywhere at all, I suppose."

Maylou poured the coffee.

"Bubba Morris, instead of having your ears taped back, we should've had your mouth taped shut instead," Doris said. "That's the biggest mistake we ever made, wasn't it, Vern, not having his mouth taped shut?" But Vern kept his eyes downcast and Doris sighed.

Just then CeCe came to the screen door and told Bubba that little Larry wanted him to come tuck him into bed right away, and Oscar too. CeCe stood there with her hands on her hips like the whole world had to stop and wait for her. She was peering into the periwinkle trailer trying to see as much as she could.

31

"I want my dog back," Maylou said under her breath to Bubba. But CeCe heard and spoke through the screen.

"He's hardly your dog, sweetie, and besides, little Larry's quite attached to him. They always sleep together, it's the cutest thing to see. That little wiener dog gets right under the covers beside Larry, and they sleep that way like pint-sized twins," CeCe said.

"I want my dog back," Maylou said straight to Bubba.

"I'll get him," Bubba said, swallowing taffy and heading for the door, which he exited through. Maylou could hear him outside fighting with CeCe over Oscar's fate before they moved into their next-door trailer.

"Honey," Doris said, "Larry's but four, why don't you let him keep the dog? Oscar's his best friend, it seems."

"Because I'll poke little Larry's eyes out with my pinky fingers before he gets to keep my only canine accompaniment," Maylou said. She was the one who'd rescued him as a pup from the clutches of evil in the first place. She was the one who'd taught him he was a dog, not a guinea pig, when she'd found him in the cage among the others over at blind Beulah's. It had been disheartening to see him eating lettuce and guinea-pig pellets like it was the right and tasty thing to do, and for the longest time. She'd helped turn the brow-beaten mongrel lightsome and happy-go-lucky. It was her gave him his zest, and plus, his carnivorous tastebuds. She'd deprogrammed him like it was some cult he'd fled from. To this day lettuce had pull. Oscar was brainwashed at an early age and had to be reminded that life was a cabaret, a kooky privilege. Dance like a butterfly, sting like a bee, she told him. Get while the getting's good. Waste not, want not. Maylou turned and smiled at Vern. Vern jumped at the smile, and grinned. Doris sighed.

"Well, I guess we better go," Doris said. "We'll pick you

up for church tomorrow at ten."

"Church?" Maylou said and glared at her sad father.

"Don't worry, we're not Holy Rollers or anything like that," Doris said, trying to lighten things. "If that's what you thought. But, Maylou honey, now's a time when a little prayer is needed, don't you think? Besides, you'll like it: it's the drive-in church in Indian Rocks. You won't even have to get out of the car."

Maylou figured she'd better knuckle down. She was going to need a map to know her father. When they were alone, she set the can of black cherries on the kitchen table between them along with two bowls and two spoons. She heaped some cherries into her own bowl and pushed the can closer to her father.

"We hit the jackpot with mama," she told him. "Now things won't be as rosy. I hone for a charmed and simple life. Consider me a shoo-in for your rebounded affection. I will weather the storm with you on my back. I will sprout wings and fly you home. In my voice hear the rustle of sky, feel the meticulous beauty of flight."

Maylou ate a single cherry and spit out the pit. Since it looked like her father wasn't going to help himself, she dished some into his bowl for him. She put a spoon in his hand and with it poised over the cherries he said, "I don't know which way is up. I don't know if I'm coming or going. My bones feel weighted with lead. It's not very nice the way I'm feeling."

He took some of the dark fruit into his mouth and father and daughter regarded one another as they worked to separate the pits from the flesh of the matter.

"It's like your mama and I were swinging from a lofty trapeze," he went on. "I can picture her in sequined cape, plumed headdress, her thigh muscles hard and oily, her hands chalky with powder for firm grip. Like two sparkling birds we swooped under the world's big top, blowing kisses midair, knowing well the sure grasp of ankle, the delicate clutch of wrist. But now I've fallen through the safety net, down through to the sawdust ring below the tent's heavenly dome. Your mama's kisses are sent to dead air that encircles me like a cold wind. I miss her hot breath on my neck, the brush of our lips, the beat of her heart in my ears rolling like thunder as we passed in flight, skimming the earth like two birds of paradise."

"That's some picture," Maylou said. "You and mama as show-stopping birds on the flying trapeze. Some becharmed romance." That night, Maylou and John laid separate in their own darks. Maylou felt like a child again, back under her father's roof, at home but not at peace. She felt old though, too, in a new and sad way. She was wakened once or twice by the sound of the air-conditioner grinding and thumping across the room, and while waiting on sleep to come retake her, in the quiet behind her eyes, saw her mama clear as anything. She saw her father there too, standing next to her mama but somewhat less clearly. Then way pushed off to the side, Maylou saw a girl so small it took a long time to recognize her as herself, the teary cheeks as her own. The good and comforting thing though was that her mama had her arms out ready to scoop her up. Her mama's eagle eyes were so dead-set on her that Maylou had the feeling that even if she shrank away to nothing, her mama would find her, just root her out and give her sugar and sugar on top.

The Drive-In Christian Church in Indian Rocks had a lineup a mile long. Vern's beaten-up Olds was crowded with Vern, Doris and Bubba in the front, and John, Maylou and Oscar in the back. Maylou could tell Oscar had to pee by the way he wagged his tail and climbed all over her, so when a man a few cars ahead got out to let his beagle pee, Maylou got out with Oscar. It was no problem since the cars were hardly moving at all, and Oscar seemed so relieved to tinkle on some buttercups that any inconvenience was soon forgotten. They got into the car again and Oscar sat on John's lap.

The drive-in church was a stucco and wooden structure with an overhang under which the cars drove. The front of the church was not much to look at since all the action happened at the back. The parking lot for the cars looked exactly like a drive-in movie lot, but bigger by far, being both wider and deeper. In the distance, where the car lot ended, was a field full of picnic benches where the churchgoers could have lunch afterwards and chat or witness to one another. There were a few trees on the edge of the field, but mostly it was either grass or pavement.

For all the lineup, Vern got a not bad spot eight rows back from the pulpit. There was a huge, brown cross and a lectern and some TV cameras and lights set up.

"Well, for once we'll be able to see the preacher," Doris said. "It's Reverend Hessop this week; he's supposed to be very handsome. Not that you'd care," she said, elbowing Vern. She was in a good mood in her Sunday best. Maylou couldn't see much through Doris's hat, anyway, which was decorated with a salad of fruit and flora. Looking into the cars around them, Maylou saw that most of the women had these same hats on, or similar. There were also any number of kids still in their pyjamas, with games and dogs. Some couples had brought a thermos of coffee and some finger foods with them to eat while they enjoyed the sermon.

For what seemed like ages, scratchy gospel music was piped into the car, while the congregation waited for the last car to take its position. Doris and Bubba both sang along with many of the songs. Thankfully, "Amazing Grace," as sung by Elvis Presley, was not played in such a way as to ruin it forever for Maylou, and she was grateful.

When the preacher did come out, he spread his arms as wide as the cross, and yelled, "Welcome, my little lambs, to the only drive-in church in Indian Rocks, in the state of Florida, in the United States of America. Amen." During this Vern was scrambling to turn down the volume, and Doris was poking him with fervor.

"Good Lord, Vern, I'm deaf now so as I'll miss the rest of the sermon. You might've known it would be too loud the way you had it set. Well, that just spoils it all for me," Doris said and crossed her arms. "We may as well just go home, except that we're trapped in here."

"Sorry, pet, it was my mistake," Vern said.

"Well, it wasn't God's or the Reverend's, that's for sure," Doris said.

The preacher was saying that they were going to start with a hymn and that the congregation could either sing along or toot their horns to the music. "Honk for Jesus," he said.

"Honk, Vern," Doris said and reached across Bubba and started honking out of beat.

"Let me, mama," Bubba said, "I like this part."

This cheered Doris somewhat and she smiled back at John and Maylou. John was asleep. Oscar, who was still lying on his lap, was quietly chewing the end of his leather belt.

The service went on with the people being told to clap their hands and raise their arms at various points. The raising arms was difficult in the cars, but everyone made a valiant attempt. Maylou looked into the surrounding cars and saw folks trying to raise their arms and still keep their coffee from spilling. There seemed to be a lot of arguing going on between husbands and wives, and the kids in the back seats. It didn't seem worth it, considering that when God looked down from Heaven he would see only different colored roof tops, and none of the pious people inside waving like crazy to him. He'd probably think it was a supermarket lot, or a shopping mall. Maylou got out of the car.

"Where are you going?" Doris quipped.

"I'll be back," Maylou said and slammed the door.

"Wait, I'll come," Bubba said, edging over Doris.

"No, you won't," Doris said pushing him back. "You'll burn in Hell in front of all these people who'll be angels with wings spitting on you, and it still won't put your fire out. You'll be burnt to a crisp, with no one to blame but yourself. Sit down, Bubba. Vern, tell him to stay put."

But Vern was honking as though he were possessed by some beauteous spirit, and the car shone with it regardless.

Five

"HOME IS WHERE THE HEART IS, MAYLOU," John said while they were waiting for their orders to come at the Rib Barn. They'd spent all afternoon packing up Flossie's things, dividing them into separate bundles for Maylou, Doris, and charity. Some things were garbage, and those things pained. Like Flossie's toothbrush and her nitro heart pills, the plastic pantyhose-filled eggs scattered around her mama's drawer like it was a lingerie nest. Maylou had a hard time throwing them out.

One thing she wasn't going to throw out, though, was Mildred, the donkey figurine her mama had placed on a doily on top of the TV. Maylou had made it herself in school by pinching clay into the right shape and then hard-baking it in the art room's kiln. Much later, she was embarrassed at ever having given her mama such a sad and sorry present, and had tried throwing it away. But her mama had pulled the donkey from the garbage and set it right back out again. She'd told Maylou that she loved the little figurine Maylou had crafted with her own hands, treasured the hand-pinched burro and the thoughtfulness that went behind it. Mildred, her mama said, was as sure a sign of Maylou's devotion as ever there could be, since she'd taken the time to make something for her mama's delight instead of making something for her own childlike purposes, which she could have just as easily.

Looking at the figurine now, Maylou saw it not so much as a sign of her love towards her mama, but as a sign of her mama's love back for her. The fact that her mama'd bothered to keep the donkey in the first place, had dusted and looked at it affectionately all this time, moved her. She planned to display Mildred somewhere at home in Topeka as a symbol of the love that went on between them, a tad strange though it was, but still true enough. Love works in mysterious ways, Maylou thought, it comes in small packages, and is as blind as reputed.

John couldn't come anywhere near clearing things out for reasons Maylou understood. If you want to trample a man's heart just put him in the room he once shared with his wife and close the door. Leave him alone with the White Shoulders still soft in the air, new sheets sunny-fresh on the bed the way they both liked them. Let him see the bookmark two-thirds of the way through the novel she was reading, the nightdress hung flimsy over the chair. Leave him to remember the feel of her. The twenty years of trying to make a baby and failing every month of all that time.

Maylou had seen young mothers pushing their babies through the mall in strollers, the infants crying at the top of their lungs, so hard their chests heaved and their tongues vibrated. The mothers never did a thing to help, just kept looking in store windows, drinking from take-out cups. They didn't stop to do the simple and small thing the babies were hollering for, which was to be fed. To be held to breast and sheltered from the world, quenched with warm milk, a fist-small stomach to be completely filled. What a terrible ache such a scene must have caused her childless mama who would have let go and fed those babies as if from her own soul, if she could have.

Maylou imagined her mama back at home laying down across the bed. Her father would come in and lay beside her, hold her tight from behind. Mostly she'd cry into the pillow, her hands cupping her empty breasts, until the light had all gone from the sky. John knew his wife, knew she was crying for babies she wished had been born to them, babies that weren't hers to comfort or smooch, and that he hadn't been able to give to her. Maylou thought her father knew the sound of her mama crying for babies the way he knew the sound of a clock ticking, or any other cry of nature, raw and undeniable.

When she first opened her mama's closet, the sight took her breath. There were the pantsuits and coordinates so familiar. The little white cardigan her mama would throw on if it was chill. The straw handbag on the shelf, reserved for Florida along with the sunhat for flea markets. Maylou held tight the closet door for fear of falling down, like she was living a nightmare. Her mama. She'd lost her mama.

John had seventy-four years, to her own twenty-six. It was her mama Maylou went to and it was her father she was left with. John, who was near to stone deaf, shy and private. Though there was never a thing he wouldn't do for her. He would buy his daughter whatever she wanted, drive her here and there like a taxicab with no meter. Talking to her, understanding her cares though—he wouldn't even think there was a need. She loved him but, and he loved her, and now they were alone to make their path in the chilly world. Maylou would have to be marble-hearted the next while, hold onto the gist of herself.

"Daddy, I guess tomorrow we better plan on heading over to the Crematorium. We can't put it off another day, though a cakewalk it won't be. All those papers from the Largo Medical Center are sitting up on the highboy in the bedroom. Then after that I guess we better pack up and get a move on for home. Zak'll be anxious."

"What about Oscar?" John said. "What're we going to do about him?"

"It's pretty clear that Oscar still grudges me wedding Zak. There's no love lost between us, so I think I'm going to give him to that little Larry kid next door after all."

"That'll be a nice thing. They're best friends, those two. Poor old Oscar."

"Never mind, daddy, we can get us another wiener dog sometime, if we want. I like the name Woody or Buster for a dog now. Lady or Inez. I never thought Oscar would live this long anyway."

Just then Myrna, their waitress, arrived with their ribs. As she set the plates down, John's teary eyes locked hers.

"My wife's just died playing cards," he said. "Just like that, with no warning at all. We didn't even know it, we thought she was laughing. What a thing. We used to eat here, my wife and I did. Frequently."

"I am sorry," she said, turning to Maylou. "Were you her daughter?"

"Yes," Maylou said, shy.

"Well, you two eat up and if there's anything I can get you, let me know," she said and started to leave.

"Thank you," Maylou said.

"We'd been married forty-seven years," John piped. "You never know, do you, when it will happen. You can go just like that. With the flick of a light switch. Life is a heady perfume. But in the end, a mixed blessing."

Myrna wanted escape.

"You read about things in the paper, but you never think

it will happen to you," John said. "Terrible things happen to people. Hard-boiled criminals with dark places inside them try to get even. They have hearts black and swarmy as weevils, and more gripes than you could count on all your fingers. They were raised in a world blissless and lacking perks, without so much as a soft towel to wipe the tears from their faces, swigs of hard booze their only comfort. As adults, their concerns don't jibe with society's. They've been known to drive drunk onto curbs and run down children playing in the grass in front of their houses. They've made convenience-store operators beg for their lives and then have shot them in the kneecaps for no reason but they could. They have peculiar beefs. Used to be evildoers were sent to Alcatraz, but that's all changed. Now inmates are fixed up with radios and TVs, their cells are like swank bachelor pads. *60 Minutes* gives them airtime to boo-hoo their plights and spew oily-tongued speeches about the hard lives they've lived, and what they're now owed by the rest of us, society's good eggs. Bully, is what Flossie would say to them. At least it was a natural cause took my wife, and fast, the way many wish death would come. We can be thankful there was no suffering," he said. "None at all."

"That's right," Myrna said, "we can be thankful for that." And she sped off.

After supper, they stopped at the Publix in the Sunshine Plaza and then at Walgreens for Maylou. Both places John told the checkout girls the sad story of his lost love.

Back in the trailer, they decided to hit the sack early in preparation for their trying morning at the Crematorium. Maylou was sleeping on the pull-out in the living room, and John kept the small bedroom in the back. Oscar was around somewhere, but stayed scarce. During the night, Maylou heard Bubba and CeCe fighting, the sound carrying in through the walls from next door. It ended about four a.m. when Bubba slammed the door and drove away in the Olds. CeCe cried loudly for a while and then the light went on. Maylou snuck a look and saw CeCe sitting at the kitchen table holding a steaming mug of something. Behind her was Vern, braiding her long, pale hair into a tight rope she could hold onto.

In the morning the Olds was back and CeCe's hair fell in waves. Maylou and John were both wearing black when they came out from the periwinkle trailer, Maylou carting Oscar, ready for the Crematorium. Next door CeCe was sitting on the front steps, sipping from the same steaming mug as the night before. In the yard, Larry was dropping what looked like rocks into some water in a pail, which he was stirring wildly with a wooden spoon. He had an apron on over his denim pants that said "I love West Virginia," the love implied by a red heart. He looked very small and sweet bent over the pail like that, and Oscar went crazy to get to his side. Maylou decided to ditch the dog right then and there.

"What're you cooking up, Larry?" she said and went over to have a look at what was stirring in the pail. It took her a minute to make out that it was beetles, large, dead, blue-backed beetles, that Larry was stirring round and round in the water. She counted seven of them.

"Umm, that looks good," she said, "I'll have to get the recipe from you sometime." She smiled at little Larry and then at his moody mama. But CeCe wasn't paying attention: she was way off somewhere else in her mind.

"What do you call that fancy recipe of yours anyway, Lawrence?"

"I call it Beetle Soup," the boy said, his stirring slowing just.

"Maybe I should try some out, before I go and make it up for my daddy's supper tonight," Maylou said.

Oscar was sitting at Larry's feet. His eyes were hazy and wise as he watched Maylou making a fool.

"There ain't enough for you. Not once I give Oscar his share," Larry said.

And with that he stopped to whisper in a loud kid's way to what would momentarily become his own aged wiener dog. He told Oscar that his breakfast was ready and then he carefully poured out two bowlfuls of the water into dirty plastic planters. He strained out three beetles each as topping. There was one beetle left still floating in the pail. Larry glanced at Maylou. She could tell he was thinking maybe he could squeeze out another bowl for her but he decided against it. Oscar sniffed the water casually, drank a bit and then caught the largest beetle in his mouth. He put his head back and crunched it in half, shaking his head from side to side to ease it going down, all the while staring at Maylou, his eyes narrowed. Then Larry picked a beetle out of his soup, looked at it between his fingers, and bit its head off. He too watched Maylou the whole time.

"That little wiener dog's yours," she said and turned to get into her daddy's wood-patterned station wagon, where he was already waiting on her.

"What do you suppose CeCe's thinking of staring into space like that, daddy? She doesn't know her boy's eating bugs right in front of her."

"Butterflies maybe," John said. "She has a butterfly collection. Puts pins through their middles like it doesn't mean a thing. She's a farm girl and thinks nothing of skinning a rabbit besides. Once I saw her poke out a fish's eyeball whole. She told little Larry it was like a marble, only better, because if you bit down into it your teeth wouldn't bust. She's probably thinking about that. About fish eyes and the like."

"I heard her fighting with Bubba last night and then Vern was braiding her hair," Maylou said.

"Yeah, I've seen him do that. They fight a fair bit. I guess most newlyweds do. It was different with your mama and me. We never fought. Life's too short, Maylou, for sour words; it's way too short for ugliness."

"Newlyweds? They can't be newlyweds, daddy, little Larry's got four years behind him after all," Maylou said.

"Things don't come in the order they're supposed to every time, Maylou. Bubba and CeCe been married just on six weeks. That's when the fighting started, so Doris says. Vern says it was later. They had a honeymoon the first week, in Tallahassee. He doesn't know what went on on that."

The Largo Crematorium was pink and aquamarine with iron grilles on the windows. It had a wrought-iron double door at the front, patterned with corn husks. It looked airy and sun-bleached, like it had never intended to be set any place else but where it was at. Pecan, cypress and oak trees covered the grounds, in some places the twisted roots coming up to make mounds in the grass, in some places breaking through altogether. Climbing vines of deep purple flowers covered the walls of the building and arched over the doorway.

"This is pleasant," Maylou said.

Inside, their cremation adviser was a young man decked out in a black suit, but otherwise looking like anybody you'd see on the street. Maylou took to him, safe in the knowledge that he'd done right by her mama since he looked decent enough. John had begun crying as soon as they'd entered the man's office and seen the urns laid out for display in a cabinet behind his desk. The fact that they'd already cremated Flossie was one of the first things the adviser put across. He spoke almost in a whisper, and Maylou had to convey it louder for John. He'd been leaning forward to hear what she was saying and when it registered he jumped back, wincing. His face lost its color. Maylou carried on. She guessed that she'd known what she was in for and just wanted to get on with it. This wasn't the way she'd do things herself though, if she had her way.

She thought her mama's passing was a private matter and it wasn't sensible that all these people had to be brought into it. John made matters worse by telling everybody and his brother the sad story of the last card game, including every checkout girl he could get his hands on. Even the crematorium's secretary, RoseBelle Krahn, hadn't been spared. Maylou would have just given her their names and then waited for their adviser to come out and get them, but her father had gotten into a detailed conversation comparing notes. Turned out her husband had died recently too, after stepping on a Portuguese man-of-war while walking drunk down the beach. This had happened at a time when he was supposed to be at their son's organ recital and so RoseBelle felt both angry that her husband had never shown up at the concert, and guilty because he'd had such a good excuse for missing it. Too, he had suffered in the end from his allergic reaction to the fish's poison, quitting the world never having gained any consciousness back. Maylou overheard her father saying, "the heart-smitten are bluesworthy, and ballad material also, an ever-growing throng." RoseBelle said she got goose bumps just talking to him, found real solace lurking in his words. As a token of her appreciation, she'd given him her husband's video-tape of NFL Bloopers that had come free with his subscription to *Sports Illustrated*. She'd just cancelled the new subscription but under the circumstances they'd let her keep the bonus tape. Maylou explained to John what a blooper was, but got the idea it was still unclear to him. She'd put the tape in her purse.

To do it her way, Maylou would have quietly cremated her mama on a beach somewhere when the sun was going down. She would have played Elvis singing "Amazing Grace," plush with that heart-sad lilt of his. But as it was she just wanted to get it done, hard as that seemed.

When it came time to pick the urn, the man excused himself from the room and John and his daughter went behind his desk for a closer look at their choices. The shapes were anything from a classic Greek style to a plain box type. The materials were alabaster, Italian marble, slate, granite, silver-plated, or onyx. The prices went from very expensive to not cheap. They decided on the alabaster one in the end. The ashes would be completely sealed into the urn, so that there could be no scattering of them about. This saddened Maylou, as she thought her mama would approve the romantic notion of being sprinkled into the Mississippi River on an overcast day. But since she hadn't been brave enough to request even a handful of her mama ahead of time for this purpose, she intended to specify it for her own ashes sometime before her demise happened.

The man came back into the room with the alabaster urn already packed into a sturdy cardboard box. There was no fuss or ribbon around the box, it was plain as anything you'd see lying around. John took a deep breath and launched into a version of his tale of heartwrench.

"I have lost the one who made me melt," he said. "My wife was a Winter. She had a little chart done up with pieces of fabric dyed colors that would bring out her eyes and make her skin tone dewy. She could never find the exact shades to match those little scraps they gave her in the color workshop she and Doris went to, but still she carried them around in her purse in case we came across something that looked close. Now I have them. Yesterday I saw a blouse in a store window that matched perfectly the green one, but my wife isn't here to wear it. I don't know another Winter, not that there ever would be another one for me anyway. Doris is a Fall."

"You don't see fish mourning their dead mates this way," the cremation adviser said to Maylou. "Or cattle or any other animal, for that matter. Remorse at the loss of life is a human trait. No one else bothers with the expense of an urn for the ashes of their loved ones, either. No animal has upset the delicate ecosystem as much as man, though, and that's a sad but true fact. To err is human, to right the wrong is divine. I insist on recycling in my house—cans, jars, newspapers, all go into the recycling box. My wife says that's why cremation as a line of work suits me to a T. I don't like the idea of the earth being littered with human compost. Humans being meat-eaters, after all. Airtight jars of sanitary ashes under the earth's surface are something I prefer to think about. Saving the rain forest is our one big hope. Plant trees if you want your grandchildren to have a sleek ozone. Plant trees and wash your baby's diapers yourself. Never ever think you are too small and insignificant to make a difference. This planet is the only Eden we'll ever see."

"My wife's petunias," John said, "were so spectacular they drew stares. Every summer we'd go to Sheridan Nursery and Flossie would pick the plants she wanted and put them in a tray I'd carry around for her. She'd put a handful of bonemeal into the soil with the seedlings before covering them over in the garden. She swore by bonemeal and had a green thumb. I would kiss that thumb like it was the holy, dirty foot of the Savior if she were here now. If she were here now

I'd buy her that blouse I saw in the window, admire the cameo-like quality of her skin, the acute slope of her forehead, and then I'd put my head down in her lap and cry."

"Love like that has no beginning, it has no end," the cremation adviser said. "You are a lucky man," he told John, "whether you know it or not. You were chosen to run the whole gamut, to feel the head-to-toe torture of love. When I look at my wife I see a dream unrealized, saddle bags, and a mouth pattering trifles I don't want to hear. I am as far from her as I am from Mars, possibly farther. Every day I ask myself what I am doing waking up in her bed. Every day I think Ms Krahn, the widowed receptionist, is more and more irresistible. I live in fear of embarrassing myself and never having a meaningful climax. You at least have given and received a healthy dose of love. I would do a lot to be like you were, maybe twenty years ago, when your daughter was new and you walked down some neighborhood street with your arm around your wife's shoulders, the sky clear above you and your heart cloudless, also."

The cremation adviser shook John's hand in both of his, and Maylou carried the plain cardboard box out to the car. The man gave John a card with his name on it and John slid the card into his wallet as they walked out.

Back at the trailer community things were quiet, as little Larry had come down sick with fever. Doris and Vern were off playing bridge at the activity center, and Bubba was at the track. That left CeCe to herself on the front-porch steps. When Maylou unloaded the box from the back seat, CeCe was all eyes.

John said, "That's Flossie's ashes in the box. We picked out an alabaster urn. It's a nice one, down at the Largo

Crematorium. A pleasant place, I got a card. And a bloopers tape. I don't know what I'm going to do now," he said, and went into the pretty trailer he'd be leaving in a few days, once they'd cleared up the phone and power bills.

Maylou went over to CeCe and sat on a lower step next to her. CeCe was classy-looking, though she'd be better off if she didn't try so hard. She had nice pale hair and dark eyebrows were a plus.

"How's it going?" Maylou said.

"Not bad. It'd be better if Larry would stop puking every five minutes," she said. "I haven't had a second to spit."

"Too many beetles for breakfast," Maylou said, meaning to be neighborly, not snide.

"I guess," said CeCe, neither one way or another.

"I hear you're a newlywed," Maylou said.

"Who told you that?"

"My daddy. He said you'd been married to Bubba just six weeks."

"Six weeks, is that all?" CeCe said. "The time hasn't passed in a blaze of glory."

Maylou let that one fly.

"You heard Bubba and me last night," CeCe said. "He's got a character leaves something behind. He's dyslexic on top of it all. Means he sees everything upside down and backwards. He can't read. Not even comics, because everything's inside out. I think it's made him retarded in a lot of ways. And I'm not being mean when I say that."

Maylou was chewing a hangnail, which made CeCe check out her own fingertips.

"You know, I was thinking about that alabaster urn," CeCe said. "Are you planning on scattering your mama's ashes anywhere? I know a nice place I was thinking of. I could take you."

"They sealed her in," Maylou said. "You can't get the ashes out, but thanks anyway. I was thinking the same thing. Throwing her in the Mississippi."

"I guess it doesn't really matter. Jesus, hear that? That's Oscar puking now too. I'm never going to get used to living in a trailer home in the sticks. This isn't living, if you ask me, not by a long shot. Not by any leaping imagination."

"Why did you marry Bubba in the first place then?" Maylou asked. "If he doesn't knock your socks off."

"God knows why. You know he's got a steel plate in his head. Imagine having a steel plate in your head, like Frankenstein. I don't know, we had some things in common, what with little Larry and all. Actually, it's kind of embarrassing, the truth. One night Bubba had been saying to me how we should get married and make our lives official and we were laying in bed going over it, when this big thunderstorm came up. Well, we started going at it shortly after and right when the thunder and lightning came so did I, if you know what I mean. So I took it as a sign that I was supposed to marry him, for better or worse. How stupid can you get. Anyway, the next day we went off and got ourselves a JP and it was done like that. It's not to say that Bubba doesn't have some good points. He has these sassy ostrich-skin boots that make him look like Clint Eastwood in some lights. And most mornings I don't even have to make him coffee, he just grabs the beans and eats a hand-ful instead."

"Sounds like you had your reasons then," Maylou said.

"I notice that you have a ring on the finger in question," CeCe said.

"To Zachery. Maybe my man's not all he should be, either. He's got some good jokes. But I guess when it comes down to it I've heard them all before. He's no gold mine of love."

"So dump him," CeCe said. "Let me fix you a cup of blackberry tea, I picked the berries myself. It's no bother."

Maylou felt better about CeCe from talking with her, but it was getting her thinking about her own bewedded in a danger-fraught way. Zak didn't have a steel plate in his head or glass eyeballs or a peg leg. There was no outward reason to dump him. Though a love-cheat he was sure enough. She couldn't count the number of times she'd caught him with, or suspected he'd just come from being with, somebody else. Whenever they went to a party together Maylou would lose Zak in the crowd almost as soon as they arrived. Then on her way to the bathroom, she'd see her husband sitting with a girl on a bed in one of the back rooms. It was always the same. He'd be telling the girl about his work as a night watchman, about the close call he'd had when a kid high on hallucinogenic drugs had come at him waving a Garden Weasel, wanting to part his hair.

"But you weren't hurt, were you?" the girl would ask, her eyes widening with alarm. She'd be wearing a boat-neck, angora sweater, and a little gold chain with a heart or a cross dangling from it against her smooth throat.

"No," Zak always assured her, "no. He was just a kid out on a spree, someone who'd succumbed to a bout of bad behavior. My escape was narrow, but unheroic. The world dishes out worse. Every day, people put knives into each other's backs and twist them. In general, they renege. Every day, a dog somewhere bites into a little girl's thigh and for a moment considers never letting go."

Maylou would look at them sitting on the bed. When they noticed her, the girl would blush. Zak would smile. She wondered what she looked like standing there in the door-way. It amazed her: the endless number of these wide-eyed innocents, ripe as fruit on the vine, their lush hearts ready and wanting to believe anything.

"Wait till Doris sees all the puke in there, she's going to have a fit," CeCe said as she passed Maylou her tea. "They'll all know what Larry had for breakfast. These old cronies in the trailers are thick as thieves. They'll be whispering about him eating beetles in broth, with me looking on."

"I didn't think you even knew that's what he was up to this morning," Maylou said.

"I knew. But I figured 'spiders and snails and puppy dogs' tails, that's what little boys are made of.' Everybody knows that, so I didn't worry," CeCe said.

"I guess," Maylou said. "I like this tea."

"Bubba'll probably leather him silly when he gets back. Poor Larry. As if he's not feeling bad enough. Bubba is on the discipline bandwagon."

"I don't know how Zak'd be if we had kids together," Maylou said. "But I already have my names picked out— Aurora for a girl, and Jackson for a boy. I think Aurora is the prettiest name I ever heard for a girl. Makes me think of rainbows."

"You're thinking of auras," CeCe said. "I have a friend who can see auras on people's heads clear as day. You don't want to have a yellow one. But Aurora is close, I guess, for an actual first name. My friend is a genuine psychic-healer over in Cassadaga, the spiritualist camp. You should see her sometime, she wears all those skirts like you do."

"Maybe she could take a message to my mama," Maylou said. "Or bring one back."

"Probably she could, but it'd cost you. She might give you a discount, we could try that first," CeCe said. "Give her a sob story."

Maylou was looking at CeCe's one earring—a prancing unicorn made of silver, but with a horn of gold.

"You've only got one earring there. You're missing the other," Maylou said.

"I only had one pierced. Nobody told me it hurt like hell, though it makes sense that it would, when you think about it. I had little Larry with me in his stroller, and he was holding onto my foot while I sat up on this stool, and after the first one I howled and Larry started bawling, and the woman didn't make me pay because I wasn't about to get the other one done and put us both through that. I'm kind of glad now because you can sometimes buy just a single earring cheap, if they've lost the match. I wear this unicorn most days anyway. It's one good thing Doris bought me last birthday. Apart from the Playtex girdle which I'll never wear. Imagine buying a girdle for someone as a present," CeCe said. "I bet Vern picked out the unicorn. He would approve a purity symbol and mythological figure soaked in lore."

"I better go, I guess," Maylou said.

"Don't be a stranger," CeCe said. "If there is such a thing."

As Maylou was leaving, Bubba pulled up in the Olds and the sky clouded with thunder and anticipation.

Six

JOHN WAS BESIDE HIMSELF over his poor dead sweetheart. At night he had dreams she was calling to him to
come ride with her on the double-loop roller coaster they
had set up at Dade City. They'd get right upside down in
line with the earth, and Flossie would come loose from the
seat and fly out, crashing down away from him. When the
ride would end he'd search for her, and up in the sky he'd
find her—a star with her face shining in it. And then all at
once the stars would break free of the sky and come falling
down on him like silver glitter dust, coating his eyelashes and
hair. And Flossie's stardust would catch on the tip of his
finger and his wife would be so tiny and perfect there, smiling up at him for the last time. He would take her heaven-
sent star face onto the end of his tongue and close his mouth
around her forever. And the night would go on and on.

In no time the periwinkle trailer was packed up and filled
with mildew eaters and mothballs, ready to be closed tight.
Maybe for good. John didn't think he had the will to live
there alone, though Doris said maybe he'd be happy to come
back, once some time had passed. He might have a change

of heart. Miss the community and his hitherto happy home.

Flossie had been keen to buy a trailer as a way of actualizing a major part of her blueprint for their retirement. Other parts of the plan included daily kilometer walks regardless of the Fahrenheit scale, vigorous mini-golf tournaments played against like-minded seniors, and oodles of time set aside to master Cajun cooking.

"A trailer would be the perfect roost for us," she had told John at the mobile-home dealership. "I'm a homebody, big on cocooning, and if a trailer's fine by me then it should be more than fine by you. A leap of faith is what's required when moving to a more compact dwelling, anyone would tell you. I really want a trailer, dear. When I think of our retirement, I picture you in seersucker shorts coming out the front door of our mobile home, stopping to deadhead my petunias, on your way to the store for rice. I can't help it, that's how I like to see us. Either we buy this trailer now and Xerox the photo in my mind's eye, or we just forget about having a pleasant retirement. It's up to you."

The trailer they decided on was a big one with wall-to-wall broadloom and a living room that expanded to the square footage of a real house. There was always a savory smell coming from the kitchen where a jambalaya or gumbo would be simmering on the stovetop. It had no temporary feeling and was as far a cry from a cramped, snail-back of a shelter as a trailer could get.

"Living here is jim-dandy," Flossie said a few weeks after they'd moved in. "I feel we have never been chummier or closer to our dreams. The air smells constantly of Roses Roses, and the water tastes sweet as wine. Wherever we go now, we can drag our pretty house behind us, with relief and one of those special hitches. We are like happy clams, you and I. Our life is hunky-dory. Pass the cumin."

A goodbye dinner for John and Maylou was staged at the famed Aunt Catfish's on the waterfront. Doris, Vern, Bubba and CeCe Morris, and John and Maylou were present. Little Larry was left, still weak, with Oscar at home with a sitter. They ate shark bites for appetizers, Bubba hogging plenty.

"Miss Manners'd have a word or two for you," CeCe said to her metal-headed husband.

"I'm a growing man, still coming into my own," Bubba said, stuffing one back.

"Who are you trying to impress?" CeCe said.

"Well, it certainly ain't me," said his mama. "That's enough now, Bubba. You won't have room for your real dinner when it comes."

"You're worse than a baby," CeCe egged.

"What's that, Valentine?" Bubba said smoochy.

CeCe rolled her eyes.

"Maylou, you're quiet tonight. Cat got your tongue?" Doris said.

Vern looked at Maylou. "Maybe she just don't feel like talking yet," he said in her defense.

"I hope that Larry will be on his feet again, soon," Maylou ventured. "I was thinking maybe some of those beetles he was eating might've had poisoned bug spray on them. I was thinking maybe little Larry's been poisoned after all."

"I thought of that," said CeCe. "But I figured with all that puking he was doing, he probably got rid of anything he might've taken in."

"He'll live," said Bubba.

"I'm glad for that," Maylou said. "Oscar is partial to him."

"That little wiener dog's as good a house pet as any I've seen," Doris said. "You'd never know he was around half the time. How old did you say he was again?"

"Seventeen," Maylou said.

"Seventeen—well, he won't be long for this world then," Doris said. "Wiener dogs don't have a history of overly long lifespans. They croak about the same age as other minor-size breeds."

John looked stricken at the blatant reference to death. CeCe shot her mother-in-law a look on his behalf.

"How's that piña colada going down?" CeCe asked Maylou.

"Easy enough, for the first one," Maylou said.

"I guess you'll be shoving off early tomorrow—about eight, maybe?" CeCe was aiming for nonchalant.

"What do you think, daddy, does eight sound like a good time to you?"

"Eight'll be fine. Not too early, but still sharp enough to have the roads clear. That's a good time to push off," John said, and Maylou made sure she caught his eye to give him a sweet smile to help him get through. She hoped to blot out his grief with words and actions cottony soft.

"This blackened catfish takes the cake," Bubba said.

CeCe sighed. She made up her mind about something she'd been thinking.

Maylou watched CeCe fidget in her chair. She could almost see the wheels turning.

"Mind if I try a bit?" Doris said, her fork hovering over Bubba's plate.

"Be my guest," he said.

"That's so fresh," his mama said. "They must have gone out and caught it right after we ordered." She stabbed up another piece.

CeCe was planning a future life. She would get to where she could play Kitty Wells all night long and live on cherry cordials, if it killed her. She wouldn't be held in thralldom by Bubba any longer. She hoped his conscience smote him for all the nasty things he'd done to her. Even before he opened his mouth lately, she felt like telling him to shut up. She thought she might be a nicer person if Bubba weren't around to put her in the doldrums all the time. Life, CeCe thought, should be a steady climb towards things delightful. I am a flower who never gets any sun, she thought. Soon I will turn a new leaf. Soon I will make wild, impassioned honey with blue-collar bees.

"My, this is yummy fish," she said.

The next morning Maylou got out of bed on the wrong side. To boot, her face had waffle marks on it from the way she'd been pressing it in sleep. She spent a good fifteen minutes trying to get the red out by applying Noxema medicated skin cream. John drank his coffee slowly, eyeing everything one last time. Maylou had saved a cinnamon bun each for them, which hit the spot when it went down.

They loaded the back of the station wagon, and gingerly, Flossie too, rested in the alabaster urn eternal. It was when they were pulling out that CeCe came flying. Her arms were heaped with bags and she charged her head into Maylou's open window.

"Room for one more?" she said frantically, and threw her things any which way into the back and then herself in after. She locked the back doors. "Let's roll," she said.

Maylou wasn't about to drive any place.

"What're you doing?" she said. "You know we're heading northwest to Topeka, not anywheres else; we're heading back to the Breadbasket of the World. To the state whose monkey was the first in space."

"That's fine by me. Anywheres but here. Get a move on, Maylou, or Bubba's going to catch wind and put a stop to me cutting loose altogether," CeCe said, looking out the rear window.

Maylou edged forward, by no means peeling out. CeCe kept looking back and little Larry came out onto the front steps, holding Oscar in his arms. He waved goodbye with Oscar's paw and CeCe blew him a kiss.

"He's a little angel, that one. I'm going to miss him," she said. "Still, in time he'll come to realize that his mama was like a bird with a broken wing living in that cramped-up trailer home on the outskirts. He'll get by. There's enough people to take him on." And CeCe turned back around to look forward. "I have flown the coop," she said.

"I never pictured myself an accomplice to you dumping Bubba, CeCe," Maylou said. "I don't feel spry driving on."

"Never mind, hon. Pretend I put a .32 to your head and you had no choice but to," CeCe said. "I'd have blown your brains out otherwise. I might not have even flinched."

"That's a good way of looking at it," John said. "I believe that's what I'm going to think, Maylou."

"There, you see. John, hand me that state map you've got up there," CeCe said. She spent several minutes poring over the map. Maylou kept checking the rearview, expecting to see the Olds any second with Bubba at the wheel. But when he didn't show up, she thought what kind of love is that; she wondered how far Zak would drive after her. And at what speed.

"Maylou, here's something. We could go to Cassadaga on our way north, and see my friend, the one I told you about. Try and contact your mama," CeCe said.

Maylou looked over at John to see what he thought, but he was watching telephone poles passing and hadn't heard a peep.

"Daddy, CeCe's got a friend who's a mystic and can let

us speak to mama again, maybe. What do you think?" Maylou said upping her volume.

"What is she? A gypsy?" John said. "I don't believe in gypsies, they bring ill luck. Though their lace making is fine."

"John, you wouldn't mind if Maylou and I went ahead and had a try," CeCe said, "just for fun and games?"

"I guess," he said. "It's on route?"

"Pretty much," CeCe said. "As the crow gets there, with maybe a teensy dip in our beeline."

Seven

CASSADAGA TURNED OUT TO BE a sleepy old Florida town set back in some woods where you'd never find it, unless you knew where to look. The way there, CeCe had been reading from a drugstore paperback, chunks out loud, that moved her. Maylou noted CeCe was into sex and hard-nosed femmes fatales. John seemed into that too, and had no trouble hearing. CeCe got his mind off his worries, Maylou handed her that.

The town was a spiritualist camp by name, and had gates harking the entrance on either side. It'd been founded in the later part of the nineteenth century by a Yankee fortune teller who was told by afterworld spirit guides to take the train as far south as it would go, and set up a winter base for a religious association from Cassadaga, NY. Legend says that George P. Colby got off the train and walked for two days straight, hacking his way into the virgin wilderness until the spirit guides Seneca, the Philosopher, and the Unknown, told him to stop. He founded the psychic center smack where he was standing in 1875, thereby fulfilling a childhood prophecy and ensuring the spirits beamed on him.

Inside the camp it was a sanctuary of quietude. Medita-tion Parks were available in which to rest or find peace of soul. Clapboard houses with tin roofs were scattered on narrow, winding dirt roads that went up and down gentle hills, heavily treed. The houses were painted personable colors and had old cars in the yards. Each house had a signpost by the walkway that said Rev. somebody and what their specialties were—spiritual healing, medium counseling, channeling, tarot, crystal ball or aura reading. In order to set up inside the town's gates the reverends had to be approved by the board. Those who set up beyond the gates were not recommended to visitors, as they hadn't been tested out by a camp official for ESP aptitude and awareness. They also weren't subject to the same camp taxes and membership fees, and so were seen as psychic groupies and misbelongers, and hard feelings went back and forth.

There was a Cassadaga Pentecostal church where weekly meetings were held on subjects like Protecting Your Karma and Astral Dreaming. The church also acted as an information center for tourists, of whom there were many. From all over the United States, as the flyer told. Inside the church there was a phone directory of resident psychic reverends, and a pay phone you could call from, to make sure they were willing and able to connect. There was a limited bookstore set up with every Edgar Cayce book ever written, and every Shirley MacLaine. CeCe had a ball, though she'd seen it before, showing off to Maylou. She told Maylou how Cayce'd been ahead of his time and was practically a god in some circles, or an extrasensory hero, at any rate.

CeCe and Maylou left John outside a store that sold dog food and flags, where there was a nice bench for him to sit down on in the sun. He took over reading CeCe's paperback and looked like he didn't have a care in the world. Which was a lie, but it looked that way. Maylou went into the store to make sure that it was all right that John sit out there for a while, without having to move on. The guy behind the counter looked like a creep, but maybe he'd just gotten dressed in too fast a time and hadn't seen a mirror anywhere around to check in.

"I wanted to make sure that my daddy can sit on that bench for a while," Maylou said. "I have an appointment that he doesn't care to come to."

"That bench out there?" the guy said.

"Right outside this front window. Is that all right?" Maylou said.

"I can't say because I don't know," the clerk said.

"Take a guess. I can live with your guess."

"I suppose then," he said. "Tell him to go on ahead and sit there for a while. That's just my guess, that he'd be fine to repose there a while."

"You want to spit that cowlick down," Maylou said pointing to the top of her head at the back to indicate.

"Some grease is what it needs," he said. "Spit won't do nothing."

"Push it back somehow, then. You're in the public eye, sitting behind that counter with the flags," she said. "Like the President, if it weren't for the dog food cans and dirt."

"Lot of people tell me that," he said.

CeCe's friend was down under the weather but said she'd take Maylou on as a favor that had to be repaid. And not at a discount. Her house was plain with lime shutters that were closed and padlocked from the outside. It had a fair situation near a stream.

Inside, tobacco and baby powder were the smells. WELCOME BIKERS signs were hung here and there, as were fly strips. Her name was Carleen and she had an old grand-dad watching a black-and-white TV with no sound in the corner of the parlor. He had a lap blanket Maylou admired for its stitchery, even from where she was at. Carleen seated Maylou and CeCe at a small table with a cover on it and a lamp. She took up CeCe's palm. She kissed it, then held it against her cheek. And then she brought it down.

"CeCe, you'd be safer having a skill to fall back on," Carleen said. "Sign up for a correspondence course in interior decorating or computers or such. That's by mail, I mean. The road ahead is rocky, minus Bubba."

"It wouldn't take too much attitude to see that, Carleen. After all, you think I cherish the idea of living the rest of my days a divorcee?"

"There's a man you'll meet, I'll call him Whiskey Sour for the drink he favors, a big man with a pitted face. He'll give you that curly-headed baby you've been pining after. But I can tell you now, there'll be nights with the moths beating against the screen door and you looking out into the dark, waiting for him to come back, thinking he never will. But he's your man for the taking and he'll love you enough. Just mind you curb your tongue at times," Carleen said.

"I don't get your drift," CeCe said, though Maylou had the idea she did.

"That's a viper's tongue you're housing in your mouth, is what I mean," Carleen said. "Sugar that snake down. A little candy floss spun round your words is what you need. More flies are caught with honey than with vinegar, which is something you ought to've learned by this stage in your development. Since you haven't yet, I'm telling you now as the gospel truth not to be ignored."

"So I'll have my baby with a head of curls," CeCe mused. "My heart's so mixed over little Larry: what's in it for him?"

"The way is unclear. But I would venture that Larry'll progress at a rate suited to a kid with Bubba's brain matter in him," Carleen said.

CeCe narrowed her eyes before she perked somewhat. "Can you get a message to Maylou's mama in the afterworld?" she said. "That's what brought us to your door in the first place."

"Give me your hand, child," Carleen said to Maylou. She rubbed Maylou's hand, kissed it, bit it, pulled each one of its fingers and tapped it against the table.

"Hm," she said. "Maybe it's too soon after. Maybe it's that I'm not myself at present. Either way, I'm at a loss. Chicken blood is what we need."

Carleen went and got a mason jar out of the refrigerator. On it was a specialty label, with a cartoon picture of an apple-cheeked woman in a chef's hat drawn in beside the printed words, FRESH FROM MOM'S KITCHEN. In the blank space below, BLOOD (TINY'S), had been penciled in.

"In case you're from the SPCA," Carleen said, patting the jar, "you should know that no chicken died giving me this blood. My friend Cordelia Naxe-Yoon lets me prick and partway drain her chicken when my blood bank dwindles. In exchange, I transmit a few words between her and her dead sister who drowned at a summer camp for co-ed pre-teenagers. Mostly, I think, they spend their time talking about boys they knew. Boys who've long since married, moved away, or come out from the closet. Cordelia leaves with her eyes moist with girlhood yearnings, her secrets just surfacing under dark lashes. And the chicken, for his part, soon recovers."

"We don't give a hoot about chickens, Carleen," CeCe snapped. "Do we, Maylou? Chickens are the last thing in the world we care about. Maylou is here to dial up her mama without having any heavenly operators disconnect her again, capish?"

Carleen shot CeCe a salty look, then focused on Maylou. She said, "I'm going to draw a little heart on your forehead with chicken blood. That's to let the spirit world know it's a loved one we're trying to contact." She dipped her finger into the jar and drew a perfect crimson heart on Maylou's brow. "Close your eyes now, child, think of your mama standing in a white mist holding her hand out to you. When you're ready, when you can picture her clearly, enter the whiteness yourself and let it envelop you. Take the hand your mama is offering. I will envision the same thing. Chicken blood usually works aces.

"Relax, breathe," Carleen said to Maylou. "Imagine your lungs are clouds filling with air, drift high, higher. The light is bright, you can hardly keep your eyes from closing it's so bright. Your mama is ahead of you, drift higher still, up into the clouds. There. Your mama is surrounded by the brightest light of all. She is engulfed in white, in pure illumination, diaphanous, billowing white, the color and feel of silence. Take her hand, Maylou. Take it now."

After a moment had passed, Carleen said, "Well, shoot."

"That's all right," Maylou said. "I think maybe I didn't see her hand clear enough in all that fog. I think maybe I didn't have a good enough grip on it."

"No, it was me," Careen said, handing Maylou a Kleenex to wipe off the blood. "My transcendental duct's been blocked all day. Tell you what we can do, though. There's a wishing well out back. Get old granddaddy to spit onto both sides of a nickel for you, and then throw it into the well. Make a wish that your dead mama will come and have words with you on our plane sometime soon. That well is way more spiritual than me," Carleen said. "And so's granddaddy, though he don't like to show it off in front of company."

Maylou wished her heart's entirety on the nickel and threw it into the well, waited for it to hit rock bottom. Her hands were shaking like they'd been doing off and on since her mama passed, along with the whole rest of her body. Even when Maylou tried thinking about something other than her mama's death, her mind keened to the loss and sent a secret message to her limbs to quake and quake, shake her all up. Maylou felt like a love junkie going cold turkey. She'd throw every last nickel she had on an easy fix.

Back outside the flags store, John was asleep on the bench with the paperback fallen to the ground at his feet. The sun shone down reflecting off his glasses, the way it did his wedding shoes, so mint and nappy years before.

Eight

THEY WERE HEADING NORTH on I-75 when CeCe got a bug up her nose about postcards. She was in the middle of writing one to send off to little Larry who, though she'd washed her hands of him, was perched up front in her mind and couldn't be shook free. She was chewing Big Red and the car smelled sharp.

"When I first saw this postcard," she said, "with the sand dollar picture and the true facts poem, I thought little Larry'd be partial because he's got one or two sand dollars at home in with his shells on his bedside table. They were store-bought by Vern, not found off the beach, though that doesn't make them any less authentic, to my way of thinking, or Larry's, I guess. Somebody had to find them sometime. He has a little starfish too. And a seahorse with no eyes, all dried up and ready to snap in half. But the more I look at this card, the more I think I picked wrong. Larry'd probably rather have a crocodile or a shark picture card. This one's too old for him. He's but four. They don't make worthy cards for four-year-olds. I guess the rule is you're not supposed to leave them behind in the first place. Nobody'd ever expect that they'd get cards, because who would send them? Nobody would think that it would be their mama sending them a card from some place other than where they were at to get it. That's why you can't find a nice one when you try. And you know if you are looking, it's because you've left your baby all alone behind you, with people you have no time for in your life, so at least you want it to be a nice card you're sending back as a remembrance. One they might keep for a while and stick up somewhere."

"You should file a complaint," John said. "You've got a point in all that." And then he said, "But you know, CeCe, maybe the right thing was done. That sand dollar is a post-card Larry'll grow into. Maybe it's too big now, but in a few years it'll fit him just fine and I bet he'll like it well enough in the end. Enough to stick up."

"That gives me some faith," CeCe said. "And I did compose a nice little message for him on the back. I put, GET VERN TO READ THIS: right at the top so's it couldn't be missed. 'Dear Larry, hope you are fine. I have flown the coop in order to better myself as a human being and get away from your daddy, who if it wasn't for that thunderstorm I never would have married, and wouldn't have ended up living in a trailer with. Maybe this is a bless-ing dressed up as something else, we'll never know. Or maybe we will. I miss you and all your small clothes I've washed so often. And you. If Doris is mean, tell her I'll come back there and slap the snot out of her. (If she's read-ing this, don't think I won't.) Your daddy wouldn't know a good thing if it came up and kissed him on the lips, so don't pay any attention to him. Stick by Vern, he's your best bet. Love CeCe.'"

Maylou nodded and kept her foot down.

"I can buy a stamp from one of those machines when we stop," CeCe said. "They're a rip-off but I'm not about to start my new life a tightwad."

"That's right, suck to your guns," John said.

CeCe got out a pad of paper then and started scribbling something else. Since John was hungry, he and Maylou checked out billboards passing. A 76 truck stop would go fine, they figured. After a few minutes, CeCe was crying so loud in the back seat they had to ask her.

"What's with you, CeCe? Is it regret come up sudden?" Maylou said.

"It's not regret. Not after the way Bubba done me, the good-for-nothing. It's just I was making this list of things I want in my new life. This nice list of things," she sniffed, "I want and won't get."

"Let's hear that list," Maylou said. "Why don't you read it out loud for us to hear."

"All right, but it's not complete and it's just how I thought them up, not in the order I plan on attaining. It might seem mixed to you."

"You could put it alphabetical," John said. "That's always smart."

CeCe met Maylou's eyes in the rearview. Then she read: "A Spanish comb for my hair so I can wear it up, a new paperback, a pocket Instamatic, some dinner plates, a pincushion, a radio, deck of cards, two ice cube trays, apple jelly, fingernail clippers, pink socks, a lamp, a box of cherry cordials, a guitar, soap, screws or thumbtacks for hanging things, Wind Song perfume, that tanning cream that does you without the sun, a bird, a birdcage, stamps. That's all so far. But it would be a start," she said. "With those few odds and ends you could make a start.

"One thing I see now," CeCe said, "is starting out on a new life you make promises to yourself the same as resolutions on New Year's Eve. They aren't a lot different when you live through them."

"Look, a Kentucky Fried Chicken," John said, pointing hopefully out beyond the highway.

"But, John," CeCe stopped him. "You don't want to grow female breasts, do you?" She was leaning forward talking into his sound ear.

"No," he said. "Not one bit."

"Then don't turn off, Maylou. Keep on going. I read this newspaper article once about a man who sued Colonel Sanders because he used to eat there all the time and breasts grew on him like a teenage girl. Turns out there are pure women's hormones in that secret recipe the Colonel dreamed up. You have to eat there three times a day to notice, but it can happen. Well, it did happen in fact," CeCe said, "to that man. His wife couldn't put blame on him though because she obviously wasn't cooking a food storm herself, so what did she expect." CeCe leaned back.

When they spotted the 76 ball on a pole some distance ahead, relief went all round. CeCe was glad of the gift shop, the pecan pie waiting, and the ladies' room. She put her shoes on, combed her hair, pouffed her nose in a small mirror. They were stiff-kneed when they stepped from the car and walked like old ducks in a line, across to the truck stop.

CeCe hit the gift shop first. She bought more Big Red, a handful of Snickers, a tape of hillbilly music, and a post-card of the ocean with a pelican flying past. The bird had a fish in its mouth, dead or alive.

They ordered what they wanted. Partway through, John got ants in his pants and kept looking out the window at his station wagon parked in the lot. Twice, him looking made Maylou and CeCe turn and look. When CeCe ordered dietetic fruit cocktail instead of pecan pie for dessert, John left the table. Maylou thought headed for the restroom.

"CeCe, I was thinking that you were strong to abandon

your lone offspring the way you did," she said. "Leaving Larry like that, waving on the front steps with my ex-dog in his clutch. You being brave as Laura Secord or Joan of Arc."

"Jesus may smite me, but thanks," CeCe said. "To be frank, Maylou, what's done is done. I can be glib, looking back, but I believe Carleen was right. The road ahead will be pitted, minus Bubba. Right now though, I think I'm wearing a lucky horseshoe as a choker."

Just then John returned, hiding something behind his back. His face was flushed. He sat down and put the little leather zipped bag on the table in front of him.

"Look what I found in the men's room resting on the sink," he said to CeCe. "I checked with the girl at the cash and she said I could keep it. Finders keepers, losers weepers, the girl said."

He unzipped the bag and took out a pocket Instamatic camera. CeCe's eyes got big and green with envy.

"It has film in it," he said, showing CeCe the numbers. "A roll of thirty-six, I bet. Just like what you wanted on that list you were making up. An Instamatic to record your new life with." He gave CeCe the camera. His hands were shaking.

As the camera passed Maylou, she caught sight of a small American flag sticker, peeling, and familiar, at the bottom corner. Her eyes shot to her daddy.

"It's on the ninth picture," he said, pointing. "That means you've got twenty-seven to go before you have to pay."

"John, can I really keep this?" CeCe said. "You're a doll. I'd kiss you but we're in public." She held the camera against her heart, then practiced the eyepiece, looking around the room at the lonesome truckers bent over their pies.

"You can tick that camera off your list now," John said, swelling. "You have a nice one of your own, so there won't be any more crying from the back seat."

"I think we're charmed together," CeCe said. "We should get a bag of fortune cookies and read them all at a stretch. We should go to the racetrack and buy lottery tickets." She reached over and fleetingly held John's hand.

Maylou didn't know what it was, but they seemed to cheer each other. What happened when CeCe developed the film would be another story. How would she like to see Doris and Vern, Bubba and herself, maybe? Flossie, late of this world, smiling on.

That night they pulled off into a Payless Inn. CeCe was already asleep in the front seat with the Recline-O way back. She'd bought a micky of vodka at the ABC Liquor and it was half drunk in her lap. Maylou wasn't having any while she was driving, nor John, though he was thinking he might have a nightcap later to make his own happy hour.

Maylou and John got a room to share and CeCe paid for a room of her own. The rooms were side by side on the sixth floor and looked out over the parking lot and the highway and a Stuckey's, where they planned to go for breakfast the next morning. Maylou's had a queen-sized bed to share.

She had a steam-filled shower and put her nightie on, thinking about Zak not being there to take it off. She came out of the bathroom when John was but halfway dressed. He stood with his back to her, pyjama top on, trembling on one leg as he stepped with the other into the bottoms. His legs were skinny and white, his buttocks bony. A man frail as that shouldn't have to stand one leg at a time, Maylou thought. Old flamingo, with a heart blue and reaching as the tide.

"Look here, daddy," she said, "they have one of those SlumberAid gizmos hooked to the bed. LET ITS MAGIC FINGERS LULL YOU TO SLEEP, it says on it. For a quarter."

John got into bed while Maylou went for the quarter. Then she got into bed beside her time-worn-smooth daddy and dropped the change in. The machine gave the same motion as the car they'd been driving all day. Maybe it was so travelers would sleep thinking they were getting closer still to where they had to be. John held onto Maylou like a wife while he slept. She looked at the ceiling like a wife too, waiting for the day to break the sky in pieces.

After a while it began to rain and Maylou went to the window. The rain pounded down onto the station wagon below. In the dark, it looked like a hearse and Maylou felt for her mama, cold and damp in the moonlit urn. She pulled her coat on and ran down to the wagon. She freed her mama from the box and kept her under her arm, inside her coat, next to her heart. Maylou thought of all the times her mama had brought her in from the rain, had changed her clothes and given her something hot to drink. Easy comfort gestures that told Maylou she was being watched over, and stopped any deep-biting chills from getting anywhere near her inside, feeling self.

Back on the sixth floor, Maylou was shut out. She wiped the wet from the alabaster urn and knocked on CeCe's door. CeCe opened in babydolls. She looked at Maylou and what was left of Maylou's mama held in her arms.

"I got locked out," Maylou said. "Wasn't ready to count my mama as luggage after all, so I went down to get her. That wagon looks like a hearse when you see it from up here. Looks just the same as that, be hard to tell them apart even for a prize, I bet, from here."

CeCe went to the window.

"Too bad we didn't have ourselves one of those RVs," she said. "I was thinking John wouldn't mind sitting in the back eating a sandwich or some of those hickory sticks he likes, while we rode up front shooting the breeze, dumping on all those two-cent cities we were passing."

CeCe shut the door behind Maylou and sat on the big bed. Maylou put Flossie down on top of the TV like an ornament to her former self.

"I got some sour cream chips and Chiclets at that little cigar store before it closed, and you ought to help yourself," CeCe said. "I can't sleep on a hollow stomach without the devil coming to meet me with flaming horns. And if you're not so tired there's an X-rated movie with that Long Dong Silver starring. Probably I'll moon for Bubba, not 'cause of any like-ness, just for old times' sake. That nightie's sweet as all get out on you though babydolls is all I can weather on me."

"I've never seen a porno movie yet," Maylou said.

"Well, they don't give medals for that. You should have at least some X-rated material to your history. This one'll be pretty good to get you going. It's got twins, one with a hare-lip," CeCe said. "Imagine having a harelip and that kind of a job. It's like those men you hear about so scared to death of heights, they window-wash high-rises for a living. Macho macho men. They want to be macho men. Like Bubba in his ostrich-skin boots with the two-inch heels. My ex-urban cowboy of love."

Maylou and CeCe got under the covers and watched side by side as the movie began. Maylou's eyes would flick from the dirty dealing on the TV, to her cold blank mama and feel something not opposite of guilt. She and CeCe held hands off and on and covered their eyes or each other's eyes at times, with their palms.

"That Long Dong's got a twisted mind," CeCe said, with her hand over her mouth this time. "I've only heard tell of him before this."

"You know, it looks like he's kept all his baby teeth,"

Maylou said. "Not one is bigger than half the size of the nail on my pinky finger. Those tiny, even teeth he's got all in a row like peppermints. I guess he took on extra in some places and kept baby things in others. A man like that'd be bound to have some wrong bits to his anatomy."

"Don't he spark you at all, Maylou? Looking beyond his stunted teeth?" CeCe said.

"No, I guess. Teeth are a factor with me. Small as his, seems criminal. And that harelip on the pinker twin puts me off the rest of the way. One of them is always playing the Peeping Tom."

"Well, I don't like he keeps using the missionary position," CeCe said. "I think he shows a lack of imagination being on top of one twin or the other every second. Though that is the only thing holding me back. I'm all for Long Dong and his wily moves. I like the idea of that hot air blower he pulled out," she said. "Makes me think I could do with some fly-by-night man passing through about now. I've got tingles in all my key places. Too bad Long's on TV and not right here this minute. You and I could be the twins, toss for the harelip."

In the dark the wind came on. CeCe had the windows opened and the curtains filled like sails and blew. The smell of dirt and water, the heady smell of rain. Morning held, beyond the night's hard-core moon.

A note was stuck under the wiper blades of the wagon. The letters were cut from magazines to start, and then went on to being hand-done the rest of the way. CeCe got to it first, thinking it was a leaf or some junk floated up. It said: "Lady-bug, Ladybug fly away home. Your house is on fire, your kid's all alone. What kind of mother are you, You should be real sorry for the way you done your boy and your good man who meant nothing bad by you in the end. Who are you to judge? Larry won't eat nothing but beetles and dirt and nobody cares or washes him after. His ears is full of stuff so he can't hear his name being called. That wiener dog's going to be put down before long and likely his ghost will come back with a wrecking ball to smash in your new life. Come home and this could change. Signed, X."

CeCe rolled her eyes.

"Bubba Morris, your pranks don't get to me no more. You just take your fat, tin-headed self on home to your mama where you rightly belong," she yelled at the top of her lungs, looking around the parking lot. She dropped the note in a puddle.

"Let's go," she said to Maylou and John who were standing puzzled. Maylou settled her mama in the back seat and they were on their way northwestward.

After a while Maylou thought of something to say.

"There's one of those filling stations that gives out the free cups for ninety-nine cents. You could get some, CeCe, for your new start. And then we could try and stop there every time so's you could get enough to have people over when you get set up. Any idea where you might be headed?"

"I'm thinking I might drift by Tulsa," CeCe said, bored. "Once when I was out shoplifting with a girlfriend, she took this little black pillow with gold tassels. On it was a picture of Tulsa snapped from a ways back, at night. It always struck my eye, sitting up against her La-Z-Boy. I might see if I can get my hands on one or win one at some bingo hall. That would be nice. I should add it to my list of things I want, if I get that far." Oblivious to the byplay, John piped up, "Bubba's like me. He don't read the extra parts in books neither. He just reads what people is actually saying. Not all the explanation that goes along with. Just the actual words in quotes."

"But, John, Bubba can't read, period," CeCe said. "He sees backwards and inside out when he looks at a page."

"No, he don't. He don't see backwards," John said.

"Well, he's pulling your leg if he told you he don't. 'Cause he does. Backwards, upside down and inside out," CeCe said. "Like Chinese or worse."

John shook his head sadly, his like-minded being so put down.

"There's no point you looking the little lost puppy, John. Why do you think I traded him in?" CeCe said. "It weren't 'cause he was too perfect to live with."

"He showed some spunk following on all those hairpin turns we took and us not seeing him then or still," Maylou appeased.

"Oh, come off it," CeCe said. "Bubba's so mean he'd choke on an ice cube before it had time to melt down."

"Are you going to take your name back?" Maylou said. "Ditch the Morrises as a pack?"

"Well, I might. I sure don't think I want to swing from the family tree. Though little Larry's the fruit I helped give seed to. My sweet and sour plum," CeCe said.

"Bubba's seed too," John pushed.

"Bubba's a name getting on my nerves," CeCe stormed. "Hubba Bubba. I should chew that gum and spit it right in his eye."

"Stop the car," John said. "That's it. She's too mean-spirited for me and my wife to hear. Let me out. We'll walk back." And John had his hand on the door handle ready.

"That's right. Pull over, Maylou. Let him out. He thinks he knows so much about things he don't have a clue on. Big talk and no action," CeCe said.

Maylou sighed, her hands started up their shaking. "Daddy, you're not walking anywhere. CeCe, put a lid on your deflowering. Good Lord, it's like I'm in the car with infants," she said.

CeCe bit her lip.

"Well, John," she said momentarily, "I'm sorry after all. Turn around and I'll take your picture with my jazzy pocket Instamatic. We've got good things in our past; no use in letting Bubba come along for a ride in my fresh life too."

But Bubba followed like tumbleweed. And when they went into a Taco Bell for refreshment, he left another note under the wiper blades. This one said: "Have you gone mental? Stop and smell the roses. It ain't too late. Almost but not quite too late yet. Repent. Be saved. Yours, X."

"That creep-show Frankenstein's something else," CeCe said. She took in the parking lot like the devil was her eyes.

"Bubba, you fat huckster, come out and show yourself," she yelled. "The mysterious Mr. X, my foot. Can't you just let me be?" she said to air.

Then Bubba came out from behind a blue pickup. He came slowly.

"There you are," she spiked him. John and Maylou took a step back.

"What're you trying to prove coming after me?" CeCe said, gaining on Bubba.

Bubba's head was low. He was crying.

"What's all this? Crocodile tears?" CeCe said.

"Yo, Bubba," John called friendly from where he'd ended up yards away.

"Hey, John," Bubba said, looking up then back down.

"Read something you'd hanker," John said. "*The Guinness Book of World Records*. About crazies and oddballs and giants. Pictures you'd have a hard time believing weren't cheated. It's in the car."

"Well, I'll take it along then," Bubba said, "if you're done with it." He looked to his wife. "I got all night to read now, these long nights, just me and the radio."

"You can't read," CeCe said between clenched teeth.

"I can read," Bubba said.

"You better get to little Larry's ears or that kid'll end up deaf as John," CeCe said.

"John ain't so deaf," Bubba said, looking over at where John had gone to sit on a curb beside Maylou. John waved at the look.

"Turn those tears off why don't you," CeCe said.

"You're cold as a lizard. Are you forgetting that night in the storm when we pledged? Remember the thunder that rainy night not so long ago," Bubba fired up.

"I remember. But I'm through, though I'll send postcards like I promised. Why don't you get a hot taco to take with you on the road? Put something in your stomach, Bubba, and you'll feel better," CeCe said. "Go."

"Maybe you'll come back," Bubba said, his eyes hoping insight.

"Maybe one day I will. It'll be raining and thundering and I'll come back to you," CeCe said. "But I wouldn't hold your breath waiting for then."

"When you come back I'll read out loud to you," Bubba said. "From a tough book with no pictures."

"That'll be the day," CeCe said, her mean streak firm.

"I will," Bubba said. "But so long for now, I guess."

He walked over to John and John gave him the book he liked. Bubba drove off in the rented car he'd got to follow undercover.

"I like that spy car," CeCe said, fingering her lip. "Did you see he was crying? My ex-hubby, ex-Romeo."

Nine

MAYLOU, CHILD, it's your mama calling. I am not an angel as I had always thought I would be, but a ghost. Angels are few and far between and shine like teeth. They radiate love. They cry alone for us all and their pearly tears are your rain in the early morning. I remember morning. I remember sky. There is no day or night here. I don't hunger or thirst. I walk miles each hour and am nowhere, no time has passed. I throb and waste, my hands can't touch my self. There is no feeling in their tips. Only you call to me when your body strikes the sound of hope emptying, weeping as from the very core. But, Maylou, I am with you. I have never left.

Maylou woke up and looked out the window of the Cheap Sleep-In. Her daddy was still soundly sleeping beside her, his eyelids quivering like insect wings, a five o'clock shadow left over on his cheeks. In her dream, Maylou had seen in her mother's eyes the force of the love she'd had for her daughter. The love sparkled there like diamonds, splendid as those a queen might lay around her baby princess's throat on the day she took her first breath in the world, and lived.

While pregnant with Maylou, Flossie hadn't been able to sleep nights, kept awake with sweeping worries. She feared the things that might cause the fetus to detach from her womb too early and slide out in a red rush, a bloody show of failure. She drank the raspberry tea the midwives prescribed to strengthen her uterus. She looked down into the clear pink fluid seeped from the teabag and begged for courage, miracles natural and born full-term. Still her heart endured blind agonies and visions of harms that could come to her child. She felt she was in some danger of losing her mind. Night after night lying in the dark, she would put her hands on her swollen stomach and wait to feel the life moving beneath them. Her body felt vast as the ocean, rolling with tides, surging with coral, fine tendrils of membrane rippling. In the dark, she'd be comforted by the pulse deep within her of a starfish unfolding, awake, and brilliant with life.

Outside in the parking lot, the Cheap Sleep-In's neon sign went on, VACANCY flashed electric pink, and Maylou moved away from the window. She knew the stories of her mama's wanting her like they were written in stone. The stories were the kind of love fables that filled a child up better than food, sated even the worst hunger.

After one night at a Payless Inn, another at a Russell's Budget Hideaway and now the Cheap Sleep-In, CeCe had put her foot down. A big howl-out ensued with John saying a bed's a bed. CeCe countering not quite, that a bed's not a bed if it's tacky as Minnie Pearl. She'd pleaded to just once stay somewhere where cheap wasn't implied in the name. She'd twisted and stamped until John had shrugged like it had never really mattered to him where they stayed: any port in a storm. Even Red Carpet Inns were pushing it, CeCe had added, but John had just shrugged again, looking bored. The plan they settled was to spend the day hanging around town where CeCe'd spied a five-and-dime she wanted to mooch in and a beauty parlor where she aimed to have something radical done to her pale hair. Then they'd move on and sleep somewhere less cheap that night. No sign of Bubba. Tulsa a way gone.

Maylou's dead mama stayed heavy on her mind and she felt truly she walked a lonely street, orphaned. She and Patsy Cline. She and all those other C&W stars who knew heartache and pockets of quarters with no one to call or the wrong number or a busy signal. She would read the last-month-current *Glamour* that someone had left under the Gideon's and space out. She might get herself a Fanta and spread some Nutella on the Peek Frean crackers CeCe had stashed in her bag, and might as well forget about ever seeing again. She'd use the other end of her toothbrush as a knife to spread it on thick. She'd call Zak too, before she didn't feel like it again for the umpteenth time.

"Hey, there," Zak said when he finally answered. "Thought you'd forgotten about me. Everything under control? Some yahoo called Bubba rang up the other night looking for you. Who the heck is CeCe? Where are you at, Maylou? Is there trouble?"

"Oh, yeah?" Maylou said. "Bubba called? Bubba Morris? We're by Arkadelphia. What'd he say he wanted?"

"He wanted CeCe. Said something about wanting his misaligned wife, the prime cause of his downfall, hereafter known as the Ice Queen. Something to that effect. What's going on, Maylou? Is John there?"

"He's okay. He's sleeping. We're just waiting for CeCe to get her hair fixed. She's got this long hair she's sick of. Then we'll move on. CeCe knows herself as Bubba's fleeing ex."

"Is Flossie with you?"

"On the dresser. This nice white urn." Then Maylou cried. Tears and souvenirs, she thought.

Zak said, "Oh, darlin'," as close to the phone receiver as

he could. "We gotta get us together again. You still sound pissed at me. But I swear I'm gonna quit this graveyard shift as soon as Jimmie Ray gets back and we'll see more of each other then. I promise. And I'm gonna ask for more money and I'll buy you things. Sweet-smelling eau de colognes: a different bottle for each day of the week. A smell for every mood. Some of that Musk for the sexy times. Then Honeysuckle Rose, Orange Blossom, Charlie, Cachet, whatever you want, I've been researching. A whole parade of smells, you'll be my princess in a mango grove."

Maylou's crying spell was drying up and she thought it might be good public relations to be more generous on the phone since all these wires and poles were between them.

"Listen," Zak said. "I want you to know that Shirl's completely out of my life. In fact, she's gone. Moved away. Hey, how long can you take someone who can only cook elbow macaroni?"

Maylou was watching John get out of bed and walk across to the bathroom. Only the toilet and a bathtub were behind the wooden door. He'd have to wash his face and put in his dentures at the sink they had in an alcove in the room itself. At least the mirror never fogged. Maylou thought her father was walking dazedly, like he was still half asleep.

"Maylou, you know I'm sorry about this whole ordeal," Zak went on. "The saddest single thing I can think of is you and your old daddy driving along together for miles of endless road. It's not like he can even hear what you're saying when you talk to him. I bet you keep the radio blasting for company."

"CeCe's there, I told you. Did you make that tape for me, by the way?"

"Yep, but just about drove me crazy. It took twenty times to fill both sides with Elvis singing "Amazing Grace." I played that musty hymn till I knew it backwards and had it rewrote to make more sense."

"Good. Now I can hear it almost enough without rewinding, time'll be saved in the end. And batteries. Thanks."

Maylou looked up and John was bent over the sink, running water over his dentures. He put his teeth in and then spat and splashed water over his face, making a lot of noise and fuss.

"I better go," Maylou said, "my daddy needs to use the phone."

"John does? All right then, Maylou, hurry on back. Forgive me my trespasses, won't ya, hon? All of 'em. Be my ever-lovin' gal again, for better or worse, in sickness or in pain."

"I just kind of have mixed reviews. By the way, did Shirl ever get around to replacing that slip of mine she took? The one I prized."

"Not yet. She's gonna mail it back as soon she gets settled. She wants to wash it first. It was already packed away."

"You got to scrub it by hand. It's French. Real Rue de France lace."

"I could call and mention that."

"Don't bother. It doesn't matter so much any more."

"She might know to do that on her own, Maylou. You have to give people more credit. Shirl was a clean freak, never left the lid off the toothpaste or used a memo twice. One thing I'll say is she kept the drawers neat and the vacuum bag emptied."

"Yeah, well, ole Miss Molly Maid."

"You're still grilled. I can understand. Bound to be. Never mind though, hon, believe me, it was a flash in the pan, a thorn in my side, and now it's been plucked and put out. We'll start fresh the minute you get home. I've got some new jokes for you I've been saving up, there's one about a blind man'll have you in stitches."

"Can't wait. See ya."

"Maylou?"

Maylou heard her name and hung up anyway. It caused some fury below in her stomach. John was looking at her. He was standing by the window in his pyjama bottoms. His eyes were a way off.

"Maylou, all night I heard music. Like butterflies dancing over meadows of grass. Like fields or an ocean with waves. But the thing is I know the song, but I don't recall the words."

"Yeah, well, maybe it's the song that counts in and for itself."

John looked at his daughter vaguely with his right hand down at his side marking time and place.

"But I have a voice, Maylou. There are words on my tongue wanting to stand up and be counted. Do you know?"

"I know, 'Joy to the world. Joy to the fishes in the deep blue sea. Joy to you and me,' daddy. That's all I know. And like that bumper sticker says, HOW DO YOU SPELL RELIEF? J.E.S.U.S. Somewhere between music and bumper stickers there's words you'll like using when the time is right. The words'll come marching in surefooted when something needs to be said." Maylou checked the coins in her pocket.

"I'm going to go and get me a Fanta and sit out in the sun a while. You should wolf down some breakfast across at the Waffle House if you're peckish, I'll catch up later," she said. "Don't fret, daddy, so."

Maylou drank her pop stretched out on the roof of the station wagon in the motel parking lot. She used the rolled-up *Glamour* as a headrest. Before long a red and yellow taxi-cab pulled into the space beside her. The driver got out of the car and did some half-hearted, limberless calisthenics before ambling over to Maylou. She had a bare midriff that seemed to take his eye and hold it. Initially, he spoke to her navel but then he moved up.

"Catching some rays?" he said. "I was thinking since you've been sitting out here a spell you might've seen a badass fella by the name of Cooter Robbins pass by. He'd've been wearing a shrunk-up leisure suit with a yellow hanky in the pocket. Kind of walks like he's too good to keep his feet on the ground. Jumped out of my cab at a light with four-sixty on the meter and I've been chasing him ever since."

"It's with some chagrin I admit to having had my eyes closed against the sun for most of the time. Except when I sit to sip my Fanta, but those times are brief, especially now it's warm and less quenching than it had been previously. For the past few minutes I've been considering throwing it out behind those persimmons." Maylou was struck by the look of the cab driver whose two gold-capped front teeth shone with a light of their own even more—set off as they were by the empty spaces on either side. Again she realized the import of teeth. Zak's teeth left no impression, but these teeth were beauts.

"My name's Maylou Puce Turner, and yours?" she said, trying to make her midriff look good, which was easier to do lying flat, but then she couldn't see right.

"Renny La Pointe. Two words. Well, three in all. Maylou, I'm a straight-shooting son-of-a-shit but a nice enough fella and I would like to invite you, seeing as we're acquainted now, to dine gratis with me in the back of my taxicab as it's about lunchtime. I've got some Dixie Cups in there we can fill with lite beer; I only drink the light stuff since my old man died of cirrhosis of the liver from drinking beer instead of water most of his life. He had this fear of water, linked to sewage treatment, so it really wasn't his fault, even brushed his teeth with beer. So what do you say? Lunch?"

"I wouldn't say no," Maylou said and got the Cover Girl compact out of her shorts and powdered the sun's shine off her nose.

Renny held the back door open for Maylou, who got in and then slid over. But Renny closed the door and went around and got in the driver's seat in front of Maylou. He turned the key and put on the air-conditioning and Janis started right up partway through "Bobby McGee." Maylou fell in with it. Renny took two Dixie Cups out of the dispenser he had attached to the dash and filled them with beer from a can he had under the seat.

"Maylou Puce, I'm going to fix you one of my very own Whistling Dixies, named after the cup they ought to be served in."

Maylou watched as he took half a bag of colored mini marshmallows out of the glove compartment. He fished for green ones and dropped three into each cup of beer. Then he put the bag back into the compartment and pulled out a little blue-stained bottle of food coloring. He shook a few drops into each cup and then swilled it around. The sides of the paper cup turned blue, the beer an awesome blue-green.

"Lovely," Maylou said.

"Pour vous mademoiselle," Renny La Pointe said as he handed Maylou her cup. They chinked.

"A toast," Renny L.P. said, "to that smart-aleck Cooter Robbins who brought me your way this fine day."

They drank and Maylou took in a mini marshmallow right away. It tasted fine. They sipped, listening to the music without saying many words.

"What are you having for lunch?" Maylou asked, hoping to see him chew something with those gleaming gilded teeth.

But Renny's disposition fell. "This is my lunch," he said. "That's why the marshmallow lumps: to fill your stomach.

It's not enough?"

"It's plenty," Maylou said. And Renny whistled her another Dixie. And another.

"You know, sug, I've got a confession," Renny L.P. said after some while. "In God's eye that ain't the first time I've given Cooter Robbins a ride and he haven't coughed up a cent for it. I don't know why I keep on doing it. I must be a bigger fool in my way than my pa was. Maybe we was both born brain-dead in the sense department. I don't like being had. I don't know why I do it. He waves me down and I stop each and every time. Why don't I keep on going? Just keep on trucking."

"Some things are imponderable," Maylou said, holding out her cup to be refilled.

Renny took the cup too hard and caved in the sides as the paper had aged. He threw it under the seat and pulled out a fresh one. Now, where the clear plastic was in the dispenser, Maylou could see that he had only a limited number of cups left. Renny dropped in some green minis but also an orange one that he didn't seem to notice.

Maylou nabbed a chance to pick out the orange and push it into the crease at the back of the seat. They'd stopped using the blue dye a while ago.

"I've got another confession," Renny said. "I know why I pick up that scoundrel Cooter Robbins each and every time. It's because of his baby sister Miss Raquel Robbins whose hand is gonna be mine one joy day. She makes them delightful hankies for his pocket. I live to see the colors she chooses. That's why I started with these mini marshmallows. The colors are dead-on."

Renny La Pointe burped. "Pardonnez-moi," he said. He continued, "She needed me like air. But with every tooth I lost to decay and hard solids, she seemed to love me less.

MISS YOU LIKE CRAZY

When I had my goldies put on she told me goodbye. She said I looked too deranged to be seen around with. She said she was afraid of catching cooties if she kissed me. Frenching was out of the question, she said. Forever. She said she didn't expect to have to tell me that. That was a sign, she said, of how far apart we had sailed in life's glory seas."

"She sounds uncharitably mean," Maylou said. "I can't say for sure, but it's my guess that you're better off a SWM, that's Single White Male, as the personals would say it."

"I never got over her. I almost ran over her once. She was jaywalking." Renny ate a handful of minis with unabashed ill spirit.

"Renny, shush before things get too overly sad for me to stay in the back seat of this small taxicab."

"Raquel was the creme de la creme. Her initials were R.R., the Rolls-Royce of females I used to tell her," Renny railed on. Maylou clenched her fingers. "Sometimes she would say, 'Excuse me, Renald, I must partake of the lavatory.' Lavatory. She whupped my heart as good as Queen Voodoo herself might've done."

"Renny, why don't you come on back here with me. I have a confession too." Renny turned to Maylou slowly. His long black hair lay against his neck in wet curls. His eyes were deep pools.

"Renny, your gold teeth shine me up where babies are made," Maylou said. "You know what I mean? I want to drown myself in merciful flesh. Why don't you come on back here with me." She narrowed her eyes and tilted her head back against the seat. She moved her hand up her thigh. Renny opened the door.

He took his thing out shyly, but Maylou treated him and it special and soon they both felt welcome enough. She tried to kick off her shoes, but Renny told her to pay no mind the upholstery. Once Maylou thought she heard him whisper, "Raquel," and she said, "Hush now, it's Maylou Puce, heart."

After a final Whistling Dixie, Renny La Pointe sped off to take a senior, name of Mrs. Platt, to the Ramada luncheon buffet where her nephew was in charge of the cold salads and rolls, and where she went every Tuesday, rain or shine, come hell or high water, without fail, and planned to keep on doing so as long as she could bear to swallow that stale bread and greasy lettuce. He was, after all, like a son to her.

"Maylou, I may be the product of a broken home but, Lord, look at me now."

CeCe was twirling around doing things with her hands to show herself off like the prize behind one of the *Let's Make A Deal* doors. She had on a new dusty-rose sleeveless dress that cinched in at the waist. Maylou was feeling easy-baked and sleepy-headed from dozing in the sun the rest of the afternoon and was not prepared for the sight she met.

"Like it?" CeCe said, pleased as punch.

Maylou had to crane up to see the top of CeCe's hair, even though she was still lying on the roof of the wagon and CeCe was standing on the ground beside it. The hair went up. Way up. It spun around and around, dove in and out, over and under in a complicated coiff.

CeCe dusted the hood of the car with her hand and climbed aboard. She sat with her legs crossed, looking up at Maylou and then straight into her own reflection in the windshield.

"Maylou, I was dying to get back to tell you all about it. I'm entered in the prestigious International Super Do's hair contest: Fashionable Hairstyles for the Fashionable Lady, and

Videl thinks I'll win First, or at least get an Honorable Mention. Of course, I don't actually get anything if my do wins, but they took my picture with bare bodice—don't worry, I had a towel wrapped around me, I just looked completely naked—and it'll be on the walls of the majority of this nation's better salons within a few short weeks, I've been assured. Can I have a sip of that Fanta if you're done with it?"

"It's pretty warm by now."

"No matter, just something to wet my throat before I tell you the rest." CeCe chugged the orange liquid as best she could without tipping her head too far back, keeping a hand firmly on the pale pile for extra security.

Maylou found herself looking from the skyscraper hair way down to CeCe's animated eyes and then way back up again.

"Well, I step into that beauty parlor we saw kitty corner to the trust, Get Set Beauty Salon, it was called, where they had a sign in the window that said, 'One Stop Beauty Shop We Correct Others Mistakes Friendly Relaxed Atmosphere, Specializing in Frosting & Shading—We Know How To Treat A Woman Right,' and this elegant beautician—I found out later she was walleyed, but she hides it by compensating her head to the side, I didn't even suspect for the first half hour—shows me over to this little pink love seat with swan arms. Before long I intuit that they think I'm one of the models for the hair show. By talking to the sultriest brunette you ever saw, I gather that this means I get a free wash, cut and blow-dry, and my makeup professionally applied by a Mary Kay Cosmetics representative, plus some degree of fame which money alone can't buy. I believe, Maylou, I heard opportunity knocking with both fists. I am convinced. I had no choice but to open the door. So I'm having a smoke with the girls, some of whom had real butt-faces but nice hair, having a conniption every time Videl, the head stylist, looked my way, in case he caught me out. Soon he comes over with this book of hairdos and starts looking at us one by one, trying to see who should get what. You should have seen them fancy topnotches. Names like, 'Oh So Sauvage,' 'Spiky Gamine,' 'Will O' The Wisp,' 'Beehive Yourself,' 'Last of the Mohicans,' 'Viva La Pompadour.' Guess what this is on me?"

Maylou stared. The names were causing havoc in her sun-dried head. "The second one?" she said without conviction.

"'Spiky Gamine'? No way, Jose. 'Beehive Yourself.' This is a replication of the real thing, with some artistic license, and no bees." CeCe laughed and fondled her tower of Pisa. "Videl says I'm the honey pot. A couple of times, you know, Maylou, I thought I saw he had a boner right through his pants. Either that or a over-ripe banana in there. I've heard about real artists that they never need to have sex 'cause their satisfaction comes from their work. Monks too. Not nuns, they still want it. My girlfriend's sister is a sister, ha, and she says that's the hardest part. You would think it would be all the scrubbing floors they do, but it's not. Luckily, Videl was all business from the word go or I may not have been held responsible, seeing as how I'm a nubile bachelorette. Maylou, I feel fresh as a daisy with my new look, can't you find it in your heart to tell me I look nice?"

"Well, you look nice, CeCe. Yes, you do. You look very nice. I'm still getting used to it, I guess; these things take some time for adjustment. Cat had my tongue. In all prac-ticality though, CeCe, reasonably, how on earth are you going to sleep on that architecture?"

CeCe rolled her eyes. "Like any other normal person. I'll just take some care."

"But how will you shampoo?"

"Actually, I won't. Videl requested me to kindly wait on washing till the contest results are announced in a week or so, two tops. In the meantime I can use talc to dry up the scalp oil, he said. I've got some Johnson's Baby Powder in my bag. He's pretty sure I'm going to win and he only wants to have to do touch-ups, not whole remodeling, when the time comes. It's no big deal. I don't blame him at all."

"But you don't know where you'll be in two weeks. You're not thinking of hanging around here, are you?"

"Hell no. What do you take me for, a nincompoop?" CeCe slid off the car. "Cripes, Maylou, give me some credit." She assessed her man-made beehive in the side window. "Videl says they'll fly me back at their expense from wherever. It's all under control. I would have thought you'd be happier for me. You're not jealous, are you? Envy is a sin, right up there with murder. Well. Below murder; I'm exaggerating since I'm worked up. I didn't mean to imply a likeness or any kinship between you and Son of Sam, really. It was just luck, plain and simple. I was in the right place, at the right time, through happenstance. That little beauty shop did enspell my eye the minute I saw it, though, so destiny may have had a hand in the playing out. Anyway, I'm heading in, coming? I aim to blow this popsicle stand before John gets too firmly planted."

But within the walls of the motel, trouble had come and gone. The Grim Reaper had left his calling card in the form of the lifeless, though still lovely, Aster Van de Venter, college drop-out, on the floor in front of the bathroom in CeCe's suite. The maid's uniform had shifted to one side and tattooed above her breast, Maylou read, Sworn to Fun, Loyal to None. The maid lay in a pool of water still holding the hose of a vacuum cleaner—now unplugged. The bathtub brimmed with sorrow.

"Oh Aster," the assistant manager was saying as Maylou and CeCe approached the opened, half-cleaned room.

"What's all this?" CeCe said as she stepped over the corpse. Then realizing what she was looking at she clucked her tongue and said, "I might have expected some one thing or other would happen to rain on my parade. I am umbrella-less and completely at odds with my environment. This is the last straw, Maylou. These dumps give me the creeps. People dropping like flies, no remote for the TV, I could go on and on. It's a bottomless pit I'm looking down into. I want to be where birds sing a pretty song."

"But it was you left the bathtub running," the assistant manager said. "You are responsible, at least partly. Young Miss Van de Venter was trying to make things nice by—" he could hardly choke out the rest of the words—"vacuuming up the overflowed water. Poor child," he said. "Poor Aster, flower's namesake." He swiped at his thyroid-troubled eyes, amplified under glass.

CeCe began to pack toiletries into a bag while holding her neck stiff. Human tragedy would not spoil her better-than-average chances of winning big in the hair pageant. She would not let Videl down. This was his own maybe once-in-a-lifetime chance to put the Get Set Beauty Salon on the map. He was counting on her. Looking to her to win for him the accolades he deserved. CeCe didn't see her Water Pik.

"Poor Aster? How about poor CeCe?" she said. "Looks like Aster did some nosing around in my things before she decided to take a bath." But as she was saying this her eyes fell on the Water Pik partially covered by a tie-dyed silk scarf. Her ears burned but she didn't let on. CeCe turned to

Maylou, who now had an arm around the assistant manager's puny shoulders.

"Let us not grow weary in well-doing," Maylou quoted, "for in due season we shall reap, if we do not lose heart."

The assistant manager nodded. "I was coming by to check the fuse box at the end of the hall because the lights in the lobby were blinking on and off like something was shorting. At first I thought it was because I was hungry, my eyes playing tricks, but then I realized that they really were blinking, the lights. And there was Aster—shaking and sizzling like bacon in a pan. She was smiling real wide and I could see the new dental work she'd had done to spruce her appearance, that yellowed bicuspid a thing of history. She was humming like a refrigerator. Then limp as a rag doll she fell when I unplugged the vacuum. The humming stopped. Had I had lunch when I usually do I wouldn't have debated the lights. I would have known. You can be sure I'll do right by her."

"That's very touching, but if you don't mind I'd like to pack my underthings now," CeCe said. "So if you'll excuse me. Maylou, lasso John and let's get a move on before the roof caves in or a tidal wave hits or something. I'm going to chalk this up to experience and thank goodness we won't ever have to set foot in this flea-bitten dump again."

The assistant manager sputtered and took up Aster's leg at the ankle and dragged her safely out of CeCe's room and into the hallway, not letting go of CeCe's eyes until he had dropped the leg. Cagey as a dog with a bone. Aster for her part held fast the hose.

CeCe thumbed the manager. "This guy gives me the willies, Maylou. Get a move on, please." And she shut the door to her room behind her. Maylou looked at the closed door like it was a wooden face, hard and blank of feeling.

The assistant manager blinked, trying to process what his mind wanted not to. "There but for the grace of God go I," he said in a harsh whisper.

Through CeCe's closed door came, "Don't be so anal. Stop pussyfooting, Maylou. P-lease."

Maylou shrugged at the woebegone man like she felt sorry but had no choice but to shake on out of there. She felt numbed to any death other than her mama's most recent. Heaven must be suffering rush hour, short-order angels dishing out halos like donuts-to-go. She walked down the hallway towards her room.

The assistant manager's voice followed, "Your friend's got no call saying such things. I want you to know that JFK's flame won't be nothing to how I'll burn in memorial to Aster." And when Maylou looked back the man was down on his knees, saint-like, beside the stilled life.

Ten

CECE WAS IN A COLD SWEAT of mea culpa over Aster. She was beyond comforting. She keened to herself in the back seat while Maylou drove and John picked out "The Battle Hymn of the Republic" on the blues harp Vern had given him as a last-minute going-away present. Suck and blow and slide. Mine eyes have seen the glory of the coming of the Lord. Dada da-da da-da da-da the grapes of wrath are stored. CeCe's ululation took on the same phrasing as the battle hymn, much to her regret and deepening pangs of conscience. Glory, glory hallelujah. The Truth goes marching on.

"This is my cross," she was heard to say. "It ain't seemly what I done and I know it for all I'm worth. I am the felonious one."

"CeCe," Maylou said, "just wolf down another Snickers bar and watch the pretty sunset. Have you ever seen a day tucking in for the night as comely as this? It's like a flaming ruby-red beach ball of hope."

"God hates me, Maylou. But it's something I'll have to live with. I miss my preschooler, though. Tonight Vern'll get take-out chicken, to give Doris a rest. It's little Larry's favorite dinner, though he feeds half of it to that scrappy mammal of yours. I miss my little boy more than you know.

When I close my eyes I can feel the downy fuzz of his newborn head on my cheek, the soft spot breathing before the bones fused into a skull. His whole head cradled perfectly in my hand. In many ways I feel dazed as an iguana at noon, heartsick and just dog tired."

CeCe had affixed the habit of patting her hair all the way up both sides as surely as police frisking a criminal and this she now did. Before leaving the hotel she'd tied a sateen ribbon in a bow near the crest. This she also checked. She seemed satisfied.

"This do is sending me a splitting headache," she said, distracted somewhat from her motherly anguish. "Though I know it's becoming, the hairs at my temples and around my ears are screaming for mercy. Videl swore it would loosen with time. It's hard not to fuss with it."

"Vanity, thy name is woman," John said between blows.

"What?" CeCe said.

"Vanity, thy name is woman," John repeated, shaking the spit out of his harpoon.

"What's that supposed to mean?" CeCe said.

"I don't know."

"Then why'd you say it?"

"I don't know."

"Well, you don't know much, do you?"

"No."

"Come on, CeCe," Maylou refereed.

"What? I treat him like he treats me back. Don't I, John?"

"I guess," he said.

"You guess right." CeCe searched through her purse like she might dig to China. "Maylou or John, do you have any Tylenols I could borrow?"

"Now she wants something," John said, "she's sweet as pie."

"Go blow your horn," CeCe said. "I'm feeling peaked

and I need you to keep care of me a little. I'd do the same. Is that too much to ask? Some TLC wouldn't kill you."

Maylou white-knuckled the steering wheel. "Another hour or so, CeCe, and we'll find a place to call it a night. Put some more road behind us. We haven't been making due headway what with sleeping in and driving unhastily and frugally. We'll get some aspirin then," she said. "It's been a time with Aster calling it quits on our behalf, so to speak. Let's just nix our repining and count our many good things."

"Well, aren't you Christian-like? You and Tammy B. You put us all to shame," CeCe said. "I feel like Jezebel herself."

"Not me," John said. "I am without shame. Flossie too was shameless. I just hope she's tuning out this rotary action. It's not fit for beatified ears. Not for the shame-free of this world, and the outer world, wherever that may be. Beyond Orion. Beyond the Milky Way."

"John, are you missing Flossie so?" CeCe asked in his listening ear.

John turned to overlook her, not trusting the lack of meanness in her voice. He looked to Maylou for help. CeCe left him behind on a slow boat heading windward. He blew a couple of notes on his Homer harp. He looked at CeCe again. She smiled. He looked at Maylou. She drove. He cleared his throat.

"She was my wife," he said. "After all. She was my wife."

And he took up a fine downbeat rendition of "Nobody Knows the Trouble I've Seen," as though some more needed saying. When he was finished he made a to-do of pouring coffee from his thermos into its lid which served as a cup.

"Sugar, sweetie?" CeCe said, passing him one of her Sweet'n Lows.

John poured the little package into the cup.

"I wouldn'ta done all that," CeCe said. "Now it'll be over-sweet. You'll just have to drink it as is and know for next time." And she was back with the hand mirror, frisking her hair up and down, up and down.

John looked at Maylou. She reached out her hand and he passed the cup to her. She drank some of the coffee fast and poured what was left out the window.

"Hey," CeCe said, "watch it," when it rained back in on her.

For a while they rode in peace. They turned off past a painted billboard advertising Sherman the Uncanny—SEE AND APPRECIATE HIS X-RAY EYES—and figured they'd hole up at whatever travelers' nest they happened across. Cheap, moderate or otherwise. Otherwise not seeming likely, going by what buildings they could judge on: a closed U-Haul rental, a closed Mobile gas, a closed Erline's Bait.

"Wasn't there a sign for accommodation back there?" CeCe said.

"I thought," Maylou said.

"Looks like just a clump of cottonwoods yonder. No Hilton. Ha. Not even a HoJo's. What did I expect? You can't make a prince out of a frog. You can't make a steak out of chopped liver."

"CeCe, why don't you take a standing jump off a short pier?" Maylou said. "I don't mean to be sexist or outdated or mean but, is it that time? You are an A-One pain in the butt lately. Nobody asked you along. I don't remember sending out invitations. We were not recruiting commissaries."

"As a matter of fact, it is that particular time, though I didn't expect to flash it around in the headlines. If you don't want me along, say so. I'll get out right here. Pull over. I have not been my usual self, I admit. I have no little kid nipping at my heels. My fat husband came only so far, then took off in his rented spy car with no second thought. I have tried to keep up a front. But I am not an ox as I seem. Strangers die on me. John used to like me and now he don't. So, cut me loose. I'll just walk back to the U-Haul and wait on somebody fetching me."

"Ah ha, that explains it," Maylou said. "You are subnormal in your B vitamins. Your thiamine's behind. We'll load up and right you again. Since you're not wholly to blame for your hormonal tracks we'll try to bear it through, CeCe. Maybe you could just talk less till you're fixed."

CeCe zipped her lips shut and nodded like the silent witness.

The sky was roundly dark as a marble, and Maylou pulled on her headlights. It didn't seem they were driving anywhere but smack into the outskirts of a place unfamilial. The trees were out of H.R. Puffinstuff, with their branchy arms and minds of foul peccability. The road stopped being paved and went to dirt. The air tightened and went chill. The car thumped and banged and the steering went sideways as the tires fought to go on.

"Holy shit," yelled CeCe. "You've hit something. Pardon my French."

"Liken to be a Kamikaze rodent of some sort. I saw the glint in his eyes as he dove headlong into the churning wheels. He came from nowhere. We have been committed suicide upon. I better pull over," Maylou said.

"Topeka's gonna think we ain't coming back at all," John said.

"Well, I never heard of a city shutting down over two lost citizens," Maylou said.

"Three," John said.

"I'd hardly call CeCe a citizen. She haven't even been there yet."

"Not CeCe. Your mama. She was a citizen. A good upstanding one. A statistic they counted on. A club member who could organize a function. A blue ribbon for their district."

"I'm sorry, daddy, I didn't think. I guess I'm distracted with the dead meat under the spokes."

Maylou and CeCe stepped into the night air while John wended into "Go Tell It on the Mountain." As they walked back to the scene the harp sounded clear and full, professional.

"He's got an ear," CeCe said.

"Just one," Maylou said and they prized the joke at John's singular expense.

"It's a hapless grayish squirrel," CeCe said as they neared the little stunned body. The squirrel was panting and heaving its chest irregularly in and out; its eyes were narrowed, then wide open, then narrowed. The only blood was a small line coming out the side of its mouth. Maylou poked it. It twitched.

"It's not dead," she said.

"The rule of thumb is: if you're breathing, you're living," CeCe said, over-sarcastic, Maylou thought, given the situation.

Maylou stroked the side of the squirrel's face, thinking it felt not unlike Oscar, and about the same size per pound. The squirrel turned its head into her hand as though to lick up the lap of comfort.

"He's in shock, I bet," Maylou said. "That was quite a stunt he pulled."

"Let's drag him over to the side and get going. John'll wonder."

"I can't do that, CeCe. Since he's not dead outright he don't qualify as roadkill, and if he's not roadkill I'm going to have to nurse him back. It's my unpleasant, undeflectable duty. I will not budge on it. See that blood coming out of his mouth?"

"Maybe he bit his lip," CeCe said.

"Maybe. Or else he's wrecked down inside where you can't see what-all. That's rocky, if not fatal. Marcus Welby wouldn't eke out much in the hope department."

"Just leave him be, Maylou. We've been privy to enough death and destruction as is, our little trio. You can't help every suicidal maniac comes your way."

The squirrel sucked in big and closed his eyes.

"There, he's dead now anyway," CeCe said.

"No, I think not. I think he's napping while we battle it out."

"He's probably in a coma. He'll be a turnip if he ever comes to. What kind of life is that for a nature buff? He'll never find anything he hides, and he'll rather sooner than later die an anorexic's worst nightmare."

"I'm going to go and get the box from my mama's urn, and a blanket," Maylou said. "Don't let anyone else run him over while I'm gone."

At the car John was blowing wild and unrecognizable and Maylou got the idea he was improvising. Jamming himself to some foxy accompaniment.

"That was a squirrel hit us. He's hanging on to life, but. I'm going to put him in a box and see if he could eat a Snickers," Maylou said.

"I wasn't doing nothing," John said.

"What?"

"That wasn't nothing I was playing," he said and colored.

"It sounded fine to me. Makes a nice change from the usual hymns and such. I could hear more."

"You could? I got some more."

"Well, fine then. But I got to first retrieve my new pet, Eulon."

John was smoking again before she got two feet out of earshot.

"What're you doing?" Maylou yelled as she harkened close enough to gander CeCe in the moonlight. Maylou dropped the box she was carrying. CeCe had somehow picked Eulon up on a stick and was trying to fling him off into the ditch and trees at the side of the road. Eulon was cleaved good.

"That's my squirrel with internal bleeding you're hampering," Maylou bellowed, lunging for the stick.

"I am but abetting the death wish he himself made a pact at. I am helping to pull the plug, so to speak. To unrecoil his stubborn little life from this stick."

"Well, don't," Maylou said. But it was too late. As Eulon came unfurled he met her eyes sadly. She heard him land and roll somewhere in the blackness of the ditch.

"Look what you've done," Maylou cried.

"That should finish him off," CeCe said, hurling the stick in after him.

"Witch. Bony louse. Stump head," Maylou swore.

"Sticks and stones," CeCe said. "My self-confidence and inner beauty are all the armor I need against such uglies. Squirrels are meant to be left alone or eaten, in case you don't know. They're wild things that bite and hibernate."

"I ran him over, he was my pet to doctor. He was going to be my recipient of first-rate chivalry."

"I just didn't want to see him suffering," CeCe said. "I took positive action and this is my thanks. Well, see if I help you again."

"You'll be sorry if you help me again," Maylou said.

"Don't worry. I wouldn't doubt but Saint Francis of Assisi

is feeding him peanuts and table scraps, somewhere in the heavens overtop Italy right now."

They drove another half mile or more with the car's red engine light newly blinking as a reminder of the wrecked squirrel in their wake, and too, maybe more so, of the physically destructive nature of guilt that can dent even metal, such is its ire.

The road was a tunnel of cottonwoods that butted out the moon and let the night reign. The car stopped short just past another sign for Sherman the Uncanny. This one said, "See the Eighth Wonder of the World—His X-Ray Eyes will Astound You." And there was a crude, cartoon drawing of a man with wild hair and swirls where his eyes would be. An arrow pointed to the right swirl and said, "X-Ray." At the bottom it read, "He can't see around Corners, but he can see to the Heart's Core like an X-Ray. Solves problems. Friend to All, Foe to None. No appointment necessary. Open all year."

"Now what?" CeCe said.

"I guess we camp out," Maylou said, trying to re-fire the cooked engine with no success.

"You've got to be kidding. I'm being punished," CeCe spewed. "First a little good fortune with Videl and my updated beehive, my new dress, and then bam. Death and destruction from far and near. I wonder if Bubba's doing me voodoo? Or Doris? Or what if little Larry's killing bugs and throwing them at my picture? I'll whammy him, if that's the case. If he didn't have some of Bubba's genes and some leftover ones of Doris's, I might have brought him along. But it's like *Rosemary's Baby* or that Damien kid from *The Omen*. Of course, I'd never tell Lawrence I thought that. His eyes are probably shining red right now with the devil's light. Nah, what am I saying? He's probably fast asleep like the little cherub he is. Doris is the one throwing bugs. I'm sure it's her. She's the one watched all those fright-night movies on TV. She'd be the one to cast a nasty mojo."

CeCe started circling her finger around her head while saying The Lord's Prayer backwards, as protection. Occasionally she flicked the finger towards Maylou and John, sending a bit of protection their way.

"Thank you," Maylou said. "I feel much safer now," and she rolled her eyes. "Do we have a flashlight, daddy, I thought I might check what's under the hood?"

"Used to have one. But I don't know what happened to it," John said. "It's not where it used to be."

The sky flashed bright with heat lightning. Whippoorwills cut sharp calls against the dark in a moonlight serenade.

"Moonlight is magic," Maylou said. "I like being at one with the elements in unpopulated wilderness. No lights bar self-luminous heavenly bodies. The way the world was before Adam and Eve. Long before the Great Ice Age and construction booms."

"Well, that lightning makes me think of how Aster Van de Whatever must have looked," CeCe said. "I'm being held to feel sorry for things and I don't like it. I'm being haunted. How am I supposed to start my new life with so many ghosts hightailing it around?"

"You should be like those little monkeys," John said. "Hear No Evil, See No Evil, Speak No Evil are their names."

"Then I'd be deaf, dumb and blind, John," CeCe said.

"Yes."

"How would that help?"

John shrugged.

"Oh. Thanks for the smart advice, Mr. Freud."

Maylou got out of the car.

"Where are you going?" CeCe asked.

"I thought I heard water running. I'm going to go see."

The trees were far enough apart that Maylou could walk through them easily. The ground was hard and dry and grassy. For all the heat lightning in the sky, the air was cool beneath the trees. Soon she came to a clearing where dark water streamed into a smooth, round pond. The water reflected the night's stars perfectly as brilliant points of light. Maylou closed her eyes, then opened them again, and the movement made the stars shimmer. She took off her clothes and laid them in a pile. She was thin and pale brown. She walked towards the water with her arms spread out to her sides and as she broke the starlight, she whispered, "Mama."

John and CeCe stood beside Maylou's clothes watching her float and dip. John stripped off to his underwear and waded in slowly.

"It's warm," he said to CeCe. "Come in."

"Do I look like a skinny-dipper to you, John?" CeCe said. "Besides, I have my hair to think about. We can't all be hippies and get wet at a moment's notice. Ponder blood-suckers, why don't you."

CeCe wandered back towards the car.

Maylou helped John float by holding a hand under his back. She walked him in slow circles since nowhere in the pool was it so deep she couldn't stand. John held his body stiff but let his legs fold back into the water. He liked the rush in his ears whenever they turned. He liked the breeze on his face. He liked knowing that his daughter's hand would not let him slide under the surface. His daughter could hold him up with one hand, with one finger, and he would let her. He wanted to float with her directing and turning him because he didn't care which way he went. Maylou walked her daddy around in circles and circles ever tightening.

CeCe came back with some drip-dries to rinse out in the pond. She hung the satiny teddies and babydolls on the dark tree branches to dry and there they floated in the night breeze like seraphim. Maylou and John had built a small fire and were holding their hands over the flames.

Maylou was thinking about her mama's body burning to ashes. Not ashes to ashes. Not dust to dust. Her mama had never been dust. Though dust was all she was now, beautiful dead bones. Maylou remembered her mama's angina pains. She had once lain down in the middle of a day, the blinds drawn against the sun, the window shut against noise though the room was breathless. Maylou had stayed beside her mama then, crawled in under her arm and placed her cheek on her mama's chest. Let my heart be the one that beats, she'd said. Let me be the one to pay the price. But still her mama's heart had stopped.

CeCe was messing with her pocket Instamatic. "John, does this thingamajig have a flash on it?" she said, turning the camera this and that way.

"I believe it does," John said, and pretended to examine the camera before turning the green "ready" light on. "All set," he said.

"Well, actually I was wondering if you might take my picture," CeCe said, "with my new hairdo to send to little Larry. Won't he be surprised and relieved to see the proof of my well-being hit home by this snap. He won't have a clue where I am. They know I'm not a camper by nature."

John stepped back and aimed the camera. Then he moved back farther. Finally he turned the camera lengthways and, from a fair distance away, managed to capture a very tiny, beaming CeCe with a bit of neck at the bottom of the picture and a whole beehive of hair to the top of the frame, threatening to continue on beyond.

"That's a good one," John said. "Looks just like you do now. Would make a nice passport picture if you were leaving the country."

"Where would I go?"

"Could go anywhere. The world is small and spins fast. You have no idea how fast when you're just sitting here. You'd be motion sick if you heard the numbers." And John looked up at the night sky, willing the whole galaxy to hit home.

CeCe awoke early to a cool morning, red sky. Her head felt pincushioned with sharpened bamboo sticks, the pain made her eyes water. She prayed for compensation in the hair pageant: Third wouldn't cut it. Maylou and John seemed unbothered by the dew that glistened on their faces and slept on. CeCe took her washing down from the trees and headed towards the car for a Snickers. She felt wildly hungry and wondered if maybe she still had that tapeworm she'd caught off little Larry. It made her stomach turn to think of it. She peed behind the biggest tree she could find, forgetting that her one foot was slightly downhill until it got damp and she had to move it somewhere without losing her balance. Camping was for the birds and convicts who were used to filth.

A tall, dark hombre was leaning against the station wagon smoking a rough-looking hand-rolled cigarette. CeCe's scalp pounded miserably.

"Hey there, 'morning," he said. "Thought I'd bring you by some Coke-Colas and fortune cookies I had leftover from a get-together I hosted a while ago. You sleep all right out there? Must've been nippy at best."

"I would've slept better in a pup tent. You are who?" CeCe said, semi-hiding her damp babydolls.

"Sherman," the man said. "I live back in there the other side of the road. I saw you wayfarers this morning when I went over for my wake-up dip. I didn't expect no others to be there so I decked out in my birthday suit. I vamoosed it back and grabbed the Coke-Colas on second thought."

"The Uncanny? Like the sign?"

"That's but a stage name formality. Just call me Sherman and I'll answer you," he said. "Sherman's plenty." He handed her a Coke.

"So what uncanny things do you know about me right off?" CeCe coyed, accepting the Coke. After all, this was a big man and she was practically a divorcee.

"Well now, I got to tune in first," Sherman said. "Really, the mind reading is only a part-time specialty. Most of the time I'm head lipstick-namer for Revlon. Mauve Over, Sunset Strip, Think Pink are some of mine." He smoothed back his hair. The man's skin was pitted, CeCe noticed, and he'd never heard of sunblock.

"Well, rev up those X-rays, mister, you've got a customer. How much does this cost, by the way? You should touch up those old signs on the highway if you expect people to find you and pay what could be a decent living out here in the woods." CeCe blinked demurely.

"I should warn you that the things I tell you will be in no judicial order, though often I see deeper and deeper as we go, and sometimes when I see into your heart the Truth can be painful. Stop me at any time if you're uneasy. Okay?"

"Okay, go on. Go ahead." CeCe showed him scrutiny. Carleen always had to look at her palm first.

Sherman closed his eyes. CeCe guessed that his X-rays could go through eyelids too if they worked right. "Spumoni's your favorite ice cream, pinochle's your favorite card game, you have some of my Think Pink in the cosmetic bag you stole from Doris. Speaking of Doris, you were the one broke the lazy Susan, not little Larry like you said, and bad news. Do you want to hear the bad news?"

CeCe had paled seeing that he could read her like a book, smack dab page for page. "Go ahead," she said through her teeth.

"Videl's in jail. Three to five for passing bad checks. He'll get max. Due to public outcry, his salon has been forced to withdraw their entries from the Fashionable Do's pageant. You wouldn't have won or even placed, anyway. A bob from Minnesota'll take First. No sixties looks this year. Plus, if you don't unmass that beehive fairly soon your hair will fall out from the roots and you'll be bald as Kojak. Further, Videl will wend into a life of petty crime based on peer pressure from his new acquaintances in the cooler. Something else. Delphine's moving in on Bubba. His resistance is low. A thunderstorm's coming. You made your bed."

Sherman seemed to falter then. He rouged completely lobster.

"Oh, CeCe," he said. "I've been alone for so long. The things you will do to me. Cupid has taken aim. This I did not expect. A woman. A baby. CeCe, I am lame-headed with this. I see that you were foretold me. Though true, I did favor Whiskey Sours, AA has made me aware that my body is a temple best run undiluted by alcohol. What do you say, dove-tail? Think no more of hitching it back to your heart's desire, for I am it." Sherman put his hand on CeCe's shoulder.

"Hands off the merchandise, buster," she snapped. "I would have won. I know it. Bald. What do you know? You come creeping out of the woods like an insect. Why don't you buzz off? I have to think." And CeCe got into the car and slammed the door.

But Sherman, his lonely soul awakened, tapped and

tapped on the window until CeCe rolled it down, but just. He put his full lips to the crack and whispered, "Love is a festooned thing. A bespangled, muddly thing." And he left her filling her mouth with his fortune cookies, eating one after another, paper maxims and all, manic as Cupid.

Eleven

"JESUS LOVES YOU BUT ONLY AS A FRIEND." A
random sampling of Sherman the Uncanny's unpicayunish
nuggets of wisdom was available in collected form in his
chapbook entitled "Nuggets to Live By," retailing for $1.99
and displayed prominently in front of them on the dinette
table. Sherman was lecturing to Maylou, CeCe and Vera,
whose sister Erline owned the bait store, about the spirit
world and the remarkable friendliness, for the most part, of
ghosts. Then the preordained, if foredoomed, seance would
begin in earnest. The coven intended to call hither Flossie,
using their combined powers of concentration. They would
chat, see how she was making out, and give Maylou a fair
chance to say adios amiga to her astral-bodied mama.

They all joined hands and just before they closed their
eyes, CeCe airmailed Sherman a kiss that would have been
wet had it landed. She was undeniably besotted with him,
had hummed him many a sappy showtune, and favored him
more than once with the twins' ambidextrous moves as
done to blue-movie star Long Dong Silver. The maneuvers
worked—left Sherman breathless, a little sore, glassy-eyed
and intoxicated. Sherman had twice been forced to dunk
the concupiscent CeCe deep in the pond to cool off. But,

carp-like, she took to the water especially as a lovemaking bed, and didn't even notice when Sherman unsprung her soggy beehive and loosed her pale hair while they copulated one gray dawn. She couldn't get enough and cared not at all for the design of the hairs on her head. Her mind was elsewhere, pleasure-bent.

CeCe opened one eye when she felt Maylou squeezing her hand. Maylou nodded towards the center of the table where a blank piece of photographic paper was developing before their eyes into a black-and-white imprint of the ghost in their midst. When the action stopped, Sherman picked up the paper and looked at the image. It was not Flossie, not a woman at all.

"Hello, friend," Sherman said. "Can we be of some assistance?" Then he spoke softly to the gathering, "Flossie is not with us, Maylou. Another soul has sought us out. We must listen to him first and then perhaps he can lend wings to our own quest. This is the dearly departed one." Sherman turned the paper around for them to see who they were speaking to. Maylou gasped. CeCe banged her fist down on the table.

"Jesus H. Christ. Bubba Morris, what in hell's name do you think you're doing here? Enough is enough. This is a private function, now beat it. I for one did not fork over hard cash to see your ugly mug floating around the room larger than life."

"CeCe," Sherman said, taken aback by her aggression towards the spook. "Bubba has passed. He is of the phantasmic spirit world." CeCe felt a stab somewhere in the midst of her to do with Aster and the notion of sympathy, the idea that maybe she was the all-time queen of mean. But she squelched the theory.

She glared at Sherman. "Oh, come off it," she snapped. Then like she was speaking to a child, "Have you heard of mirrors? Don't be so simple. He'd do anything to get at me. He's a pain in the neck, always has been. He's worse than the Blob, getting into everything and places he has no right to be." Addressing the photograph of Bubba smiling sheepishly and wearing a T-shirt that read, I BEAT ANOREXIA, CeCe finished, "this is a paying gig, chump. Cough up or hit the road."

Little bony Vera stood up in her flowery housedress, cleared her throat, and let Bubba's voice come from her mouth. "I had a accident, Valentine. Put in my sixty-five cents for a Nehi but the can didn't come rolling out. I gave the vending machine a shake and a push and before you could say Adam's your uncle, the whole thing fell over and I was suffocated, crushed by the weight of Coke, 7-Up, Nehi and Dr. Pepper. I thought I'd drop by when I heard your voice. Larry's a bona fide orphan, I guess."

CeCe looked long and hard at Vera. Then she turned to Sherman. "Is this a joke?" she said. But he shook his head. She turned back to Vera.

"Bubba, if you're still in there, in Vera, I got two things to say to you. One—what were you doing getting a Nehi? You hate Nehi. And two—too bad you've been snuffed out, but that's what you get. Que sera sera. Now get lost."

Vera hung her head and Maylou thought how weird it was that even in a housedress she looked a lot like Bubba all of a sudden. Maylou felt a pang of sorry-heartedness for him. Good thing John was out fishing or this would all be too much for him. Especially the Vera-Bubba body swap number.

"Ha. Now it makes sense." CeCe banged the table, making Maylou jump. She leaned in at Vera. "Serves you right, mister. I was thinking to myself, who is it that likes Nehi and chain-drinks a six-pack at a time like there's no tomorrow? Someone kind of fat and dumpy. Someone I've never liked. Who could it be? And then I remembered.

Delphine. Who else? You were getting a Nehi for Delphine, you lumphead. Are her fingernails still blue and spangly? Talk about scraping the bottom of the barrel. It serves you right."

"Well, I got mine, you must admit," Bubba said good-naturedly. "And now I'm a angel. A guardian angel sent down from high to protect you and be your conscience. Delphine hit on me during a storm and with her hair smelling like a perfume factory. My animal nature took up the scent and speared her pheromones, but how. She kept playing those old chanky-chank bands on her portable stereo louder and louder till I was transported to a lusty swamp of forbidden fruit. Look where it got me. Neutered in a big way. But now you and I can be reunited and I can watch over you, even in the toilet."

"Just you wait a minute, Mr. Two-Timer. I did not order a guardian angel, and anyway you don't qualify. What I do in the toilet or to Sherman here is none of your beeswax. I am a free agent. A happy-go-lucky widow, as it turns out. Go protect Delphine or your mama. Just stay away from little Larry—I'll get him."

"I could come in handy, you know," Bubba said. "I could warn you about things that are going to happen. I'd be useful and inconspicuous."

"I've got Sher to take care of me, thanks anyway. Just you run along or fly away or whatever it is you do. Disappear. I have to get used to my new status. I'll be ticking off new squares on forms from now on. Bye-bye, Bubba. So long." CeCe waved at Vera and then on second thought waved to the photograph still in her hand. The wave ruled out loitering.

"Once I was a young man full of promise. I was an innocent, a rain-washed bud, but now I am no longer," Bubba said.

"Yeah, well. Life is tough," CeCe said.

Bubba let Vera sit her own self back down. The photographic paper blanked out dead white.

"That's better," CeCe said, turning it over to make sure both sides were clear.

All eyes turned to Vera then, whose complexion was pink and flushed, her lips more red than before. She looked quite beautiful, pure and born again. Just made love to. Sherman put his arm around her frail shoulder.

"Thank you once again, Vera, for allowing another soul's energy to enter your body unpestered. It was enlightening for us all. How do you feel, a little tired perhaps?" Sherman was now rubbing her back gently up and down with CeCe watching on uncharitably.

"If I were you, missy," she piped in, "I'd go home and have a hot bath and gargle with Lysol before you catch something. This line of work could be odorous to your health."

"Not Lysol," Maylou said. "She doesn't mean Lysol. She means Listerine. Lysol's for disinfecting your toilet bowl. It's a multi-purpose household cleanser. You mean Listerine; it's a potent mouthwash that kills germs too. That's what you mean, CeCe. The one, not the other."

Vera smiled sleepily. "I think I will run along and have a nice bath. It's like watching a long, sad, foreign movie. It's hard to talk and be sociable after. Your own voice and thoughts seem so melodramatic." As she left she kissed Sherman lightly on the top of his head.

"What was all that fondling about?" CeCe said soon as the door had closed. "Did you do Vera dirty in the pond too?"

"CeCe," Maylou said, embarrassed.

"Well?" CeCe said. "Did you?"

Sherman's eyes were soft when he answered. "No, CeCe. No, my love, I did not. You, and you alone, light my fire."

And the look CeCe gave Maylou then said a lot of things,

not the least of which was, "I am the limelight. I have been lifted up, bathed by the silken fingers of time and I am miraculous. I am witchy, my hips can take a man, spin him like a top, let him go unable to see straight."

Maylou found John still fishing in the pond. He was standing waist-deep in the water, his rod steady, the line cast out from him, perfectly naked.

"Any luck?" he called.

"Seems she was unavailable for comment," Maylou said, taking off her socks and shoes and tucking the hem of her skirt through the waistband. "Aren't you cold in there?"

"I'm not cold. I haven't caught anything. Not one fish. Nothing. I was thinking about those fishing games you used to play at the carnival. 'Go Fish,' or whatever they were called. They gave you a rod with a bit of stiff string and a magnet at the end and you tried to 'hook' one of the magnetic fish they had lying at the bottom of a well of water. Sometimes the surface of the well was decorated with lily pads and bright green frogs and the water was so dark you couldn't see the masses of flat metal fish lying heaped on the bottom. You got a prize every time because they let you fish until you caught something. It never took long. The game was popular with small children who don't understand losing, and with older ones who are greedy and selfish and want something for nothing. All the parents liked it because they didn't have to console after with ice cream waffles and explanations that life is not a piece of art. Smart thinking, whoever invented that game. Not a real money-maker, but a satisfying way to spend fifty cents for everyone involved. You won yourself little colored dolls' combs, decorative toothbrushes, stick-on earrings and plastic engagement rings with ruby stones. They made sure they gave you pinkie, girl-type prizes and the boys got boy prizes. That was the thing with that game, 'Go Fish,' it didn't disappoint or surprise. There was no chance, no playing the odds, no pouting."

"No worms," Maylou said.

"Exactly. No worms." John was pleased that Maylou got his drift. "Fortune's wheel spins off-kilter," he said. "Luck is berserk and radiant."

"Bubba's dead, by the way," Maylou said. "He lost a fight with a vending machine. He showed up at the seance but CeCe sent him away again." Maylou was wading back and forth in the mud with the water smooching her ankles.

"Life ends like it begins—it just happens. Goodnight, sweet prince," John said, knowing or not knowing he was quoting someone old and English.

"I wanted mama to come, at least to say goodbye. I thought she might this time."

"Well Maylou, it's not like she's on the other end of a CB. She's probably busy looking around heaven and eating crepes. I want to tell you something with this. I want to say you ought should give up your blueprints for life. Remember that time your mama was doing laundry in the basement. She had her nightie on and she thought she might as well throw that in too while she was at it. So she was standing there buck naked when the pipe in the ceiling started leaking on her. She looked around and saw the top part of your old "I'm a Little Teapot" Halloween costume hanging on a nail. It was the teapot's yellow dotted lid and she put it on her head to stop the dripping. Just then the man came to read the gas meter. He said she was the cutest teapot he'd ever seen. Do you see? Your mama was not a teapot, Maylou. Not at all. She didn't even like tea. And here this man mistook her for a teapot. That's what life is all about. Erroneous conclusions and chance rendezvous."

Maylou eyed her father unblinkingly.

"How come I'm so knowledgeable, you want to know? I've been turned onto something deluxe. We are all of us way too literal-minded. Nothing is what it is for itself. Once you know that it makes things easy. Symbols abound, hidden in the shadows of dreams and memories, waiting to be stumbled across. The meaning of our existence is coming clear to me while I wait for a fish to bite. While I wait to hook nourishment, reel in sustenance. Remember your mama's brother with the hairy feet and gun collection? That was one disenchanted member of the human race. It is no accident that hope rhymes with grope, Maylou. We are all groping towards hope and sometimes, like your mama's brother, we miss it. He had all those guns in his house, capable weapons for any number of destructive purposes. A gun with soldier-like composure and high-tech accuracy perfect for X-ing out your life. And yet when he did take his own life it was not a gun he used, but his teeth. His own razor-sharp pearly whites gnawed through the veins in his wrist and let his blood pour out from his body. Nobody could understand why he chose that way to do it, though no one was surprised that he did it at all. A man that embittered, who couldn't bear the sight of his bare feet, had little to live for. It occurs to me now that before he could make the journey to the Promised Land he felt he had to sink his teeth into something tangible. Some last bit of life. What more likely than his own mortal flesh. It was a symbolic and fitting extinguishment that seems logical to me only at this time."

"Daddy, I think maybe you've been touched. I think maybe you've taken sunstroke or the cold water has caused havoc with your thought train. I'd feel better if you came on out of there and put your clothes on. We could roast marsh-mallows and let them glue our lips shut for a while. I'm sure this will pass."

"But Maylou, I am haikuish in clarity and expressiveness. Your mama was a fine drink of water, though her phone line will be out of service for quite some time. Like Jesus, my parables unto you are meant to show you that life is a philo-dendron, a pinky ring, a Dodge Dart, a gall bladder—what-ever you alone want it to be. We are all strangers, all family, all lost, all found. We are all doing our best."

John reeled in his line, unhooked his bait. Maylou got the idea something permanent had snapped.

"Life is a photo cube, Maylou," he went on. "Options for changing the scenarios are built-in. Revel in its splen-didness but don't trust it much. Your hand is not the only one turning things around. Other forces are at work. Read my lips—life is a scrabble."

"Come out of that murky water this minute, daddy, you're giving me a perturbation. I want you to put your head down between your knees, I'm betting your brain's been tarnished." Maylou was pacing back and forth, watching her old daddy wade his naked way to shore.

"Maylou," he said, "even a toothless chihuahua needs companionship and tasty treats. Without your mama I am a severed thing. The remaining half, the leftover portion, of an all-you-can-eat smorgasbord. I believe, though, I will come out and sit down in the shade. I believe I've said all I care to."

Twelve

"WHAT'S WITH JOHN?" CeCe said, eyeballing him through the cross vine and honeysuckle on the rusted screen.

"Non compos mentis, if you ask me," Maylou said. She was relinking a necklace with Sherman's needle-nosed pliers. "The lights are on but nobody's home. Too much open air and grief combusting in his head. What's he doing now?"

"Hard to tell, but looks like he's carving something into the bark of that tree. Looks like he's using a fork to do it. I wonder what he's up to? He's wearing a toga, seems."

"I swear," Maylou said. "Pour me another Nescafe and I'll tell you just what he's up to. He's been at the same thing all morning." The necklace she was bent over was fine and gold and had belonged to her mama. Maylou wanted to wear it as a memorial keepsake, though honestly she couldn't remember her mama ever wearing or liking it herself. Maylou intended nevertheless to treasure and point out to folks looking at her neck that it was a special something left to her in inheritance by her mama who died playing cards in Florida, in the midst of summertime's hot kiss.

She clamped the mended keepsake on with some bitterness that it was a phony thing to be doing since her mama hadn't singled it, or anything else, out in a will that could be said to be doused in abiding love. She hadn't left a will. Maylou was clinging to whatever threads of her own device she could find. She wanted some material symbol to parade the bond she'd had with her mama, besides Mildred the clay donkey. She wanted to show the depth and mutuality of their love to anybody looking. The way her father wore her mama's wedding band, or the way some widows wore black, for always and always, the color of blood dotted in the centers of their hearts, dark earth, rich around their loves.

Maylou and her mama had been close for reasons she could only guess. It may have been that she was an only child, or that her mama had wanted her so very much she'd stayed in bed the whole of her pregnancy to keep Maylou safe. Maybe it was the over-large gap in age between them, her mama knowing that by having Maylou so late in life she'd probably caused her to be on her own sooner than was usual. Birthing her child at forty-two, instead of twenty-two, had cut twenty years from their time together, and added a desperate edge to the relationship. From the very beginning, from conception even, there was a feeling that precious and few were the moments they could share. So they'd loved each other hard, pushing their emotions to the bearable limits. Separation loomed, and they held close beneath it.

"Well?" CeCe said, shoving the fresh coffee in front of Maylou. "Why is your father yonder in a toga?"

Maylou sighed, gazed out through the screen. "Near as I can tell," she said, "he's been possessed." She took a sip of hot black coffee. "All morning he's besmirched tree after tree. Each tree, my daddy says, is smarter than you and I scrambled together. Each tree has something worthwhile to contribute to the salvation of the world's community which has sunken into as graceless a state as you'd hope never to see with your eyes open. The trees, he says, speak his language.

Their native tongue beholdens nothing crummy. Like his. Now that he's enlightened, he must witness to those lesser. He must carve out each tree's message dutifully as he is their chosen vehicle. The four-pronged fork is his, and he must not stray from the purpose. It's not unlike the Indians and their totem poles, I was thinking. Those bird-bodied, man-headed, cyclops poles were what they thought the trees' inside spirits looked like. They thought the spirits looked mean and tired for the most part, as I recall, and ready to flap away. They thought God was holed up in the trees and the rest of nature too. They gave all that whittling up though, and found God somewhere simpler to get to. Maybe my daddy's reverted back to outdated Ojibwa thinking. He says when he's completed his calling, he wants to set up a turn-stile entrance above which a humble sign will read, THE FOREST OF HOPEFUL ENLIGHTENMENT—FREE ADMIS-SION.' To hear him tell it, people will line up neat as cuff links to get in. They'll traipse around reveling at so much untamed wisdom in a woodland setting. They'll exit renewed and hungry. Sher's all for it, if you haven't heard."

CeCe kept her back to Maylou, her eyes glued to the spec-tacle of John ear to bark, fork poised. "So what's he writing?"

"You won't believe it."

"Maylou," CeCe said, turning on her, "I am a *Weekly World News* subscriber. Though in my haste to ditch Bubba and for lack of one, I left no forwarding address to which future copies could be sent. Anyway, don't think you'll shock me. I've seen photographs would make your teeth curl and bleach your hair white—weekly."

"Okay," Maylou said and spewed: "DOG SURVIVES OVEN ORDEAL; TAKE THE STRAIGHT AND NARROW—IT'S WORTH THE SQUEEZE; HIT HEAVEN AND YOU HIT PAY DIRT; THE LORD SURE DOES PRETTY WORK."

Maylou blinked a few times as though to wash the print from her eyes.

CeCe raised her brow. "John might ought to have his head examined. But like I always say: to each his own. Take that Church of the Holy Tortilla in Mexico. It's in the kitchen of some plain-Jane housewife who flipped a tortilla she was making onto the floor and saw the face of Jesus looking back at her. Bubba couldn't stand the notion but I just said to him, to each his own, Bubba. That man was narrow as a rope. Narrow as a snake that dead man I married, then split from. Do you think she was a saint, or just lucky, that housewife? Or maybe unlucky, depending on how you look at it?"

"Anyway," Maylou said, with a period at the end. "My daddy's staying on here permanent; Sherman's fixing up that shed out back for him. He's going to come see mama in the Gates of Heaven and get his things when the time is right." Maylou was about to be on her lonesome.

She got thinking about when she was seven and she'd pushed her mama to anger right up to there. Maylou couldn't remember what it was she had done, but her mama was fit to be tied. Her mama had marched into the bedroom, opened the closet and pulled out a large suitcase. "That's it," she'd said. "I can't take it anymore. You're driving me crazy, Maylou. I'm so all tied up in knots I can't breathe. I have to get as far away from you as I can, some-where you won't ever find me. I'm leaving my own daugh-ter, that's what you've driven me to. I don't want to be within spitting distance."

Maylou had hung on to her mama's legs, wrapping herself around them as her mama put on her coat and pushed her way to the front door, half dragging Maylou along. She had tried grabbing the suitcase from out her mama's hand, all the while crying and begging for her to stay, swearing that she'd be good and not drive her mama crazy anymore. Maylou loved her mama and couldn't stand the thought of being without her, told her so from the bottom of her sorry heart. Her mama had arrived at the front door and with her hand on the knob, turned to Maylou, now near hysterical, and said, "Will you promise to be good and do as I say?" And after Maylou had promised, cried more like her heart was breaking, which it felt like it was, her mama had said she would stay. Her mama had said, "If you are bad again I really will leave you, and I won't come back either. No matter how much you carry on. It hurts me to feel this way."

It was when they were returning the suitcase to the closet, had kissed and made up, and were holding firm hands, that Maylou had the first inkling of the deplorable kind of person she truly was. She recalled feeling an uncontrollable urge to say something she knew she shouldn't say. She tried to hold it back but then she went ahead and said it anyhow. She said, "How come, mama, if you were really leaving me you were only taking an empty suitcase?" Her mama had stopped in her tracks, the baggage poised above her head, half pushed onto the shelf. Maylou had added, in that pause, "I knew it was nowhere you were going."

Her mama had started to cry then, and Maylou figured she'd won something. She figured she was the one in control and her mama had no clue on how to threaten her, or take the upper hand. Maylou knew this wasn't how it was supposed to be, and her guts told her she was putrid. But still she was drawn to the power play. The intense, hurtful thrill of pushing someone to breaking. Loving being loved so dangerously much the stakes were your whole heart, your emotional sanity.

"Poor Maylou," CeCe said. "Don't worry, I'll keep my eye on John for you. Brain tumor sprang to mind, I must admit, on seeing him wielding that dinner fork. Seems just when I'm hoisting my supple body from the darkness of despair and that crappy trailer park, you are being socked it to. It would have been nice for John to be your mainstay throughout, but seems he's got his own business to tend."

"This morning," Maylou said, mining for sympathy, "he took Sher's Black & Decker power drill and made a pokey hole in my mama's urn. He poured some of her ashes into the pond so she'd be there with him, and then he read a passage from the Bible, something about the spirit being weak and the flesh being strong, or the other way. He tore that page out, burned it and rubbed the ashes through his hair. Then he did some kind of two-step and bellyflopped into the water. He was wearing that selfsame wraparound sheet. There's a piece of Scotch tape now over the hole in the urn. My mama's alabaster resting place drilled imperfect, rendered spic-and-spanless by a related lunatic. I could see if it was the wending Mississippi or some such he wanted to pour her into. I could see if Elvis was singing his heart out the while." Maylou frowned and drank more coffee.

"Oh, Maylou," CeCe said, sympathetic but briefly. Then she got back to usual. "Buck up, Maylou, I've got good news I want to tell you before Doris and Vern arrive tonight with little Larry, my salvaged son. You have to be in the right mood to hear it and I'm dying to tell you, so pack up your troubles and smile smile smile." CeCe pouted. "The only other woman in the world who could possibly understand my jubilation is the Virgin Mary, and she's not here. John might snap to, Maylou. Eventually he might. Come on, put on a happy face."

"Block that loony from my sight, then," Maylou said. She knew CeCe well enough to know there was no giving attention to anything else when CeCe was scrambling for the limelight. "What time is Vern due?" Maylou said.

"Tonight, who knows. Depends how often Larry has to stop to throw up, he's motion afflicted, and how many ice teas Doris makes Vern pull over for. She has this routine she does. She complains she's parched and only an ice tea with lemon will revive her lagging constitution. So she chugs down giant ice teas and then fifteen minutes later has to pee, her eyes bugging for a rest stop. Then she's parched again, and on it goes. Chug pee, chug pee all the way home. Maybe if they come in real late and you leave real early, you'll be spared. Though that'd make Vern sad. He likes you, for some reason."

CeCe dug in her pocket. "Okeydoke. My news. Ta Da! Do you know what this is? You have to guess."

Maylou came face to face with a plastic yellow bird with popping eyes and a fluffy head of feathery hair. The bird's eyelids were hot pink, lined blue, and it had a sympathetic, if stupid, expression. CeCe shook it. Maylou looked from the yellow bird to CeCe, before taking a sip of her coffee. She watched the bird rattle in CeCe's quaking fist.

"Maylou? Do you need a hint?" CeCe pecked the yellow bird and rocked it in her arms. "It's Big Bird." She waited for Maylou to react. "Big Bird," she said, again.

"Yes, from that show," Maylou said.

CeCe spun. "You don't get it, do you? It's a present from Sher, my shiny knight in armor. But do you know why? Because our baby is growing inside my tummy this very minute, no bigger than a peanut in the shell. Can you believe it? Sher gave me Big Bird this morning and told me the news. He said there was no need for a First Response, we could save our money. It came to him in a dream last night though he can't recall if the babe had a head of curls or not—I asked. Like Carleen said, remember? My own Shirley Temple with tap shoes, and sweetness galore. He knows it's a girl. He's sure it's a girl. Sugar and spice and everything nice. Are you thrilled, Maylou? Are you over the moon?"

"Yes," Maylou said, and couldn't fit more in edgewise.

"Opal Jean is what I'm going to call her. Do you like that name, Maylou? Opal. Opal Ann or Opal Jean?" CeCe grabbed Maylou's hand in both of hers. "Well which? It's up to you, sug. Whichever you pick as a teeny remembrance of you, and our lifelong friendship, I will middle name my Opal. Am I being pushy do you think?"

Maylou opened her mouth.

"I never did believe in hula-hooping past the point. I'd give anybody a cut of my tongue at the slightest. In Sher's dream my Opal, Jean or Ann, was asleep all naked and pale and these little yellow songbirds were flying around her head. Little fragile wafery birds you could almost see through, like moons around a nova. And that was our Opal, a supernova, the brightest star there is. Sher got Big Bird as the closest thing to those birds in his dream, for when he told me the news. Not often a reformed alcoholic soothsayer tells you you're pregnant with his child, but that's something I'll have to get used to. Takes the pressure off breaking things to him. Squashes surprises like a tick under a thumbnail, though. I wish little Larry was coming by bus. Doris is a reptile in ladies' shoes."

"I hope not my mama's shoes," Maylou said. She twisted the chainlinks around her neck. "Tender Tootsies are sacred when they're all that's left of a person's walk on earth, and hold yet the shape of a foot no longer free to forge ahead."

"Well, count on seeing them shoes again, hon. Doris is no majorette for the right way to be. Her baton twirls for Number One, meaning her own self. She'll be polka-ing in them Tender Tootsies every opportunity, whether Vern likes it or not. He never was one to lead in a dance, anyhow. Vern never was one to skip to my loo, my darling."

Doris and Vern, Larry and Oscar arrived not too late that night, with the help of Bubba's ghost who gave them directions when the way was dim. His ghostly finger pointed compass-like, unwavering above the turkey claw on the dash, itself pointing to somewhere, a road less traveled.

Doris put her Louis L'Amour novel down on the kitchen table. She was pooped, she said, and full of ice tea bought from wayside diners that had AIR CONDITIONED written in icy letters on their front windows. Oscar had been skunked at a rest stop, and then doused with Aqua Velva to camouflage and was now in no mood for company. Larry held a bouquet of wild roses, black-eyed Susans, and Johnny-jump-ups for his mama, gathered from a field with Vern. He held too, a jar of murky Amazing Sea Monkeys. Vern had come down with an amoeba, a virusy thing that made him drowsy and runny of nose. He had no get-up-and-go, and seeing Bubba's ghost, however helpful, had taken its toll. Vern felt gypped in ways he couldn't explain. He was a man undone, the identifying labels ripped from his clothes, his heart an idiosyncratic, wanton organ. His hands moved randomly, his eyes searched for light at the end of the tunnel. Vern was John's first candidate for hopeful enlightenment.

CeCe pulled little Larry to her like she'd just escaped the slammer. "Let me look at you," she said. "You're cute as buttons, but a walking toothpick. Hasn't Doris been feeding you? How's that bunion of yours, Doris, anyway?"

Larry squirmed to under the kitchen table where Oscar was already lying on his side, his stout legs shuddering in a dream. Soon Larry was hand and hand with Mr. Sandman too.

"My bunion is like always, no better no worse," Doris said. The mole on her forehead looked more red and upright than Maylou recalled. "Lawrence has been crybabyish of late, and hungerless, who could blame him? A body can't have his only mama run off with only an adult-type sea-life post-card sent back as a remembrance, and not be ailed in some way. That child has had an unfunny time and with Bubba abandoning him in his way too. The child is excused. I myself have suffered big. Not only did my one son become a statistic, one of the seven Americans yearly snuffed by vending machines, but I was the victim of a fender bender outside the Piggly Wiggly just last week. I can't even repeat the whoppers that four-eyed, cross-specied frog in the other car told the law. And she paid some witness to back her up when I wasn't looking. If she thinks I'm going to have my car insurance inflated to have her little red junkheap fixed, she's sadly mistaken. I told her I'd see her in front of Judge Wapner and let him decide the verdict. Telling me it was my fault I backed out into her. I was the one going in reverse, for Pete's sake. Everyone knows it's the one going forwards who's got to watch out. She skulked off with her tail between her legs, but not before I saw a stack of Kingdom Hall flyers in the back of her lemon—turns out she's a Jeho-vah's Witness, of all things. I wonder if the manager over at the Woolworth's where she works knows about that." And Doris looked private-eye smug.

"How do you know she works at Woolworth's?" CeCe couldn't fathom she'd once lived in a trailer with this person.

"I followed her. She starts with me, I'm going to have enough ammo to rocket her to Pluto. Wapner and me'll get a good laugh when she's launched."

"What does Vern think about all this?" CeCe was in the habit of talking to Doris about Vern, even if Vern was in the room, since it was Doris answered anyway. Vern tuned out most commentary unless one on one.

"All I know is Mr. By-the-Book won't be my eyewitness because he weren't actually there. Doesn't seem to matter to him that I told him just exactly what happened. I told him why don't he go off and marry that green-toed frog and be her witness then, if that's how he wants to be." And Doris pinched her husband.

"A witness," Vern said, rubbing his arm, "is somebody who sees something, some truthful thing he doesn't want to see, so has to tell about it. All I see is lies and deceit and a woman I love despite she don't perceive daylight clear." Vern looked up only on the word "truthful."

"If I hear any more about truth and honesty and fairness I'm going to scream," Doris said. "I have never met a man so stuck in a groove like a broken LP. I don't see what's so hot about the truth. White lies are white because they're pure and helpful and good. When you look in a mirror, what you see looking back is the truth. But when someone else holds up the mirror and makes you look in it, then that's mean. Then it's like stepping on all the broken glass that mirror once was. And every minute passing lets the glass wedge in deeper and deeper till it won't ever come out, or be forgotten, since it's with you every step. Truth leaves a bloody trail, Vern. And I might add, only fools are honest. Sometimes I think you just don't get it. No one prefers daylight to candlelight."

Just then Sherman entered with an axe. Doris shut up. Vern stood.

"You must be the man with the X-ray eyes we've heard so much about and seen advertised." Vern held out his hand.

Sherman put the axe down. "I was helping John fell a tree from his Hopeful Forest. Seems the tree had nothing but profanity to contribute. There's always one bad apple, don't you find? Welcome to this neck of the woods. The washroom's straight through to the back, Doris, feel free. A body can hold only so much ice tea." Sherman smiled host-like at Doris but was met with a stiffened spine.

"Listen, Uncanny," she said, "let's get one thing straight. While I'm here you keep out of my mind. If I feel like peeing, I'll pee. And as a matter of fact I do, so I will, but don't think you can take any credit for it. I've been peeing long before I met you and I intend to pee for years to come, so don't tell me what to do. It's rude. Though you can inform me when I come back how Bubba is making out as a ghost, which is something I want to hear about. And don't make anything up because I'm uncanny too. Doris the Uncanny, isn't that right, Vern?"

Vern backed up his wife, all the while looking at Sherman. Sherman met his eyes and nodded, smiling slightly. Vern had thought, "Uncanny my big toe," and sent it Sherman's way. Vern was glad Doris couldn't read his mind and double-glad he couldn't read hers, though sometimes he wasn't so sure he couldn't. His wife wasn't so deep he couldn't get to her; it was just his air supply usually dwindled if he tried any prolonged snorkeling at her level.

Maylou laid in bed that night under Sherman's heirloom quilt in a room lit by an old oil lamp, glad for the near dark and quiet. Turns out Bubba was feeling better as a ghost than he ever had as a person, feeling more at ease with his body, svelte. Larry was destined to become a late-night talk show host and earn megabucks. Doris got used to Sherman reading her mind and did everything she could to shock him, and did. She would picture gruesome murders, fat people naked, pigs screwing. She thoroughly enjoyed her evening, and Vern was happy to see his wife smile, sometimes at him. They were happy too about Opal Jean and insisted she be raised to call them Grammie and Grumpie just like little Larry. They couldn't believe she was only the size of a peanut, their granddaughter.

John stayed outside carving by moonlight till well past the witching hour, even though his hand was so cramped he could barely move it. For a while Vern had tried to help by letting John listen to the tree, and then having him tell him what it had said so he could carve it out, but the going was slow since the trees were shy around strangers and spoke in such a whisper John had trouble hearing. Finally, he had politely sent Vern away with a promise that he would be the first person to walk the completed forest, and so be hit with warp-speed enlightenment. Vern had left also with an invitation for a dawn skinny-dip, which was John's raison d'etre and method of bathing.

Maylou held in her hand an envelope with her name written across the front in her mama's script. Doris had found the letter tucked into the side compartment of a handbag she'd helped herself to. She played dumb when Vern told her to fork it over, after she started getting ready for bed with no mention. Vern was the one who'd retrieved it, finally, with Doris saying in his ear, "Oh, that thing, you mean. Learn to say what you mean, Vern."

Alone in her bed, Maylou opened the envelope and found a letter and a photograph. The picture was old and of Flossie with her baby daughter, Maylou, on a blanket on a beach somewhere. Her mama had written in small letters on the back, "This day it rained later like I knew in my bones it would. The air was static with electricity, the way it might feel to a young girl waiting for her sweetheart to come back.

More than a storm seemed to be brewing. Everything looked like a postcard of itself, sharp and heavy outlined. It was then that I saw, or maybe felt, the future. I saw ahead to this day now, and you without me for good. Why, I don't know; it was like someone had opened a door I'd never known about and shown me a room strange but familiar too. Life is sad. It breaks your heart a thousand times when you least expect it. The air charges you electric with life just when you see ahead to the day you no longer have any life left. I waited so long for you; I hated to see the end when everything had just begun. But then you smiled, Maylou. You leaned into me the way a sunflower leans into wind."

Maylou studied her mama's face in the photograph and felt herself get cold. She wanted to take that empty suitcase from so long ago out of her mama's hand and cry that she was sorry, for her not to leave. But the drama had really happened, her mama had gone as far from her as she could get and was never coming back. Maylou still couldn't believe it. She wished there were some words she could say, some magic formula, that would bring her mama home. She didn't know why she'd ever thought she was the one in control and that her mama would do whatever she wanted her to. She just wanted her mama back, the sparkly oasis she once was.

Maylou held the letter to her lips and breathed in the faint scent of White Shoulders. Like the paper was teasing her, it carried in its fabric the memory of real arms, neck, wrists, pulse points beating strong and sending off the sweet, comforting smell of a body's living heat.

Maylou wanted to read the letter, but she held back, afraid of what it might say. She was bitter that all she had left was a piece of paper with some words on it. Her mama gone in the flesh. Words, that because they remained, were more important, more weighty, than words had a right to be. Each vowel and consonant was packed with innuendo and heartache. Fire might burn the paper, burn her mama, but the words were flame-proof.

Doris's loud whisper broke through from the kitchen. Maylou got out of bed and quietly opened her bedroom door. She could see Doris in the dim fluorescent light from the stove, spitting and gesticulating into the phone receiver. Maylou caught the tail end of what was a prank call— "There's no rest for the wicked, frog-face. That cheap costume jewelry don't fool anyone as being the real thing and you have ring-around-the-collar. Plus, bad breath and dishpan hands, put that in your Kingdom Hall flyer and pass it around. What? Doris who?" Doris hung up and hurried back to bed, flushed.

Maylou closed her bedroom door. She had her bag packed, ready to leave at dawn, Topeka-bound. Her daddy was determined to stay on and she felt peculiar going home alone when she'd come all this way to get him and her mama, both. She didn't know what to think. Her father didn't feel like her father, was what it came to. If not for the past they shared, he'd be totally foreign to her. Like CeCe was, like she was to herself. Only her mama felt like home, like somebody real and close and understandable. Maylou felt displaced, like her mama had connected her to the world via a loving umbilical cord, given her just enough slack to explore and then had tugged her back to safety. Now the cord was cut most finally and Maylou felt off-balance, like her feet lacked the essential gravity to keep them rooted on the ground. Her mama had given her a rightful place in the world and without her Maylou felt like an unwanted guest. Her mama had been home and family and self in one, easily. But how could that whole die? Where did that leave her?

Maylou looked at the photograph of the woman with dark hair, her arm around the little girl smiling for the camera. I don't get it, mama. It breaks my eye to look.

Thirteen

BEFORE MAYLOU KNEW IT she'd turned east on I-40 instead of west, heading straight for Memphis, straight for Elvis. She alone felt the sorrow that was Elvis P., the man. If he was the King of Woe, she was his Queen. Zak was a magnet to which she was not irresistibly pulled. Elvis, on the other hand, was a dynamo whose digs she yearned to tramp through, and more. Fate, she thought, had dropped her on her head.

CeCe had snuck into Maylou's bedroom early that morning and kissed her lightly on the cheek. Stay clear of lowlifes and always be hip, she'd said. Sher and I have plans to build a Florida room with chintz cushions. He is a real go-getter. I intend to live life to the fullest. I want to feel the wind in my hair.

In Memphis, Maylou headed down Highway 51 South, a.k.a. Elvis Presley Boulevard, and parked her car across from Graceland itself. The parking lot bordered Graceland Plaza with a dozen or so specialty shops, and a compound containing Elvis's tour bus and two airplanes. On the tail of the jet was Elvis's personal logo in gold letters: TCB with a lightning bolt underneath, standing for "Taking Care of Business in a Flash." Maylou thought Elvis could have done better motto-wise. She also thought Graceland was not antebellumish like she'd expected, and must have been the minimum qualifying "mansion" size.

Still, she was anxious to get to the other side of the road beyond the musical gates. After buying her ticket she was told she'd have to wait until the shuttle bus for her tour group number was ready, then she and sixteen other passengers would be transported along. She'd bought a Combo Ticket No. 2, which entitled her to a Graceland Mansion Tour, If I Can Dream (a film presentation), Elvis Up-Close (an exhibit of never-before-displayed items from the Presley collection), and Elvis's Airplanes (a film presentation about the *Lisa Marie* and an actual tour of the penthouse in the sky). About two hours and twenty minutes' worth, and about an hour's wait until.

Maylou got an information pamphlet and went into the Heartbreak Hotel Restaurant. She was thinking about heartbreak and the many hats it could wear. Elvis had broken a lot of hearts in his day. Her mama hadn't broken her heart, just taken an essential piece of it with her. A heart was like a jigsaw, made up of pieces that fit together or broke apart. Give too many pieces away or break too many, and what's left will never be perfect, never be something you should bet your life on.

Maylou remembered the way her mama reacted when she came home with her heart sore and newly tattered. Orv Begley, who drove a flatbed Ford and owned a round waterbed, had broken Maylou's heart over a slice of mocha chiffon pie they were sharing, and which she had then wept heartily into. "If you love something, let it go," Orv had said, as reason both for Maylou to stop crying, and for letting go of his shirt cuff, which she was holding onto with all her might. "I want to live by my wits," he'd said. "In life's chess game, I'm just two moves away from making it. I gotta be free," he'd said as he uncurled Maylou's fingers one at a time. "Free to be me. I mean to ramble and take my place among the sharpshooters. Try to stave off embitterment," he'd offered and walked out.

Maylou had cried and Flossie had cried with her. She'd told her daughter the first cut is the deepest and that no man would get under her skin again in quite the same way. She'd said, though, the heart could still be struck in other areas. A girlfriend might one day cut Maylou deeply, a child might, a death would for sure, and each time the pain would hit hard and mean. Apart from breathing, her mama said, that was the only way you knew you were alive. Real living hurt your bones, it made you feel you were dying.

The tourist pamphlet had a picture of Elvis on the front taken from when he was at his prime beauty. Maylou read, "Since opening to the public in 1982, Graceland has become one of America's most popular attractions. Over one half million people pass through the famous gates every year. Only at Graceland can you share a revealing glimpse into the personal life of the world's greatest entertainer.

"Hear the facts separated from the myths! See hundreds of personal artifacts! Examine the impressive array of vehicles. See the elegant formal rooms where Elvis entertained beneath the sparkle of crystal chandeliers. You'll even visit the provocative 'jungle' den where Elvis recorded some of his most poignant albums, including Moody Blue.

"Upon leaving the mansion grounds, you'll return across Elvis Presley Boulevard where further exciting experiences await you. For souvenirs, collectibles, and gifts, you'll want to browse through the many shops. You'll leave wanting to come again—for another, closer look at the incredible displays that are, now, literally the pieces of Elvis's life …

pieces which may give us the truest possible picture but may never fully explain the complexity or the phenomenon of the world's greatest entertainer, Elvis Presley."

Before boarding the white shuttle van, Maylou checked out Elvis Stuff. She couldn't resist purchasing an Elvis cookie jar, with a head that lifted off the body. On afterthought, she wished she'd bought the jar post-tour, since they were out of tissue paper and the head rattled like crazy with her every step. Walking around, Maylou had never seen so many sideburns and sexy half-smiles on men in her life. The guy driving the bus was a diehard fan and a real honey. Maylou could tell claims to fame were what kept him riding tall in the saddle. He was a sitting duck for devotional stares, as was his idol whose abode they now neared.

Turns out Elvis had acquired Graceland when he was only twenty-two years old for one hundred thousand dollars cash. That was in 1957 when "All Shook Up" was number one. Jo-Elle, the guide, said there was still a family member living in the house today, a Miss Delta Mae Presley Biggs. Maylou very much wanted to meet this old auntie on Elvis's daddy's side, who'd been living in the house since 1967. Elvis had it in his will that she could keep on living there too, as long as she felt like it. Maylou could tell Jo-Elle considered Elvis kind to a fault. Maylou hoped to run into old Delta Mae outside in the Meditation Garden where Elvis was laid to rest, or maybe by the guitar-shaped swimming pool. Maylou wanted to say, good for you, Delta Mae. Come and let your hair down, gam with me about sorrow and major loss, the way even the best-laid plans go awry. Misery loves company, and I am misery. My mama has passed. She was my best friend. I miss her like crazy. No one ever loves you like your mama, nobody would want to. All the bad things I've ever done to her are coming back to me. I am filled with shame, but she loved me anyway, knew my hurting her was my wanting to hurt myself. We came from one body—that makes all the difference. I'm pretty good at scooting around, avoiding the issues, but this grief thing has knocked me for a loop. I'm on my own now, I guess. Looks like I'm my own mama now.

In the dining room, Jo-Elle's replacement guide, who didn't offer her name, said that Elvis was a late eater; between nine and ten at night was when the gong sounded. He sat at the head of the table in order to have the best view of the television set nestled into the left-hand corner of the room. The guide believed Elvis to be an avid TV watcher and fourteen TV sets in total were located throughout the mansion.

Two things in the living room put Maylou off: the stained-glass partitions of peacocks, Elvis's favorite bird (live ones had been running around the grounds until they'd eaten the paint off the Rolls-Royce and been shipped to the Memphis Zoo); and a twenty-four-carat gold leaf, inside and out, concert grand piano, an anniversary present from Priscilla. The thing Maylou had to keep reminding herself was that Elvis was a hick from Tupelo, and in the style category the seventies ran a pretty bad race.

In the Trophy Room Maylou found out Elvis was six foot four in his stocking feet and wore a size twelve-D shoe. There was a replica of his wedding cake, solid-gold car keys, and cases of medals and letters from fans and Richard Nixon. There was a case that contained ten of Elvis's guns and over forty honorary law-enforcement badges, most of which were awarded for narcotics enforcement. That proves it, Maylou heard someone say, Elvis was no dope-fiend, I don't see a case of smack or ludes.

Outside the day had turned overcast, and Maylou's tour group mingled with others because no time limit was set on how long you could meander in the Meditation Garden. The graves were arranged in a semicircle—Elvis's stillborn twin, his mother, his father and his grandmother. Elvis's grave was center stage and was by far more flower-strewn than the rest, though Gladys Love wasn't doing badly on any account. Maylou wished she'd brought a forget-me-not or posy to say thank you for "Amazing Grace."

There was a little bench she sat on and stared at the monuments and the people passing. Live hard, die young, Maylou was thinking. In her mind's eye, she saw Elvis swimming alone in his pool, sitting alone on this bench, meditating. He had left a lot behind that kept his memory inflamed, all the songs, the rooms of stuff. His garden was full every day with people paying homage and loving him still. Maylou thought that even though Elvis had lived his life surrounded by people, bodyguards, and fans, and had probably never swum alone in his pool, he had been alone. Elvis had been as alone in his star-famed life as everyone else was in theirs, from birth until death. Didn't matter how many people were in your garden or how blue your suede shoes were. Seemed to Maylou the closest you could get to another person was to your mother. She noted that Elvis had stuck close by his mama, had let Gladys Love Presley keep feeding her chickens out his mansion's back door.

A woman with a pink scarf knotted around her thin neck plunked down beside Maylou. She sighed and shook her head. "I have a sweet tooth," she said, "just like Elvis. It's driving me wild. I used to be nuts for him. My husband was so jealous once, he snapped 'Jailhouse Rock' right in two. He said that would teach me to think twice before I said Elvis was King. My husband said in our house he was the King, and he made sure of it. I've got the bruises. This scarf is to hide the marks on my neck where he tried to choke me. This sweater hides more. My girlfriend said I've got to get myself a game plan, that's why I'm here. I want to undo the shackles that bind me and live free as a scamp. Yet I love him. Tomorrow at the Sweetheart Banquet I'm hoping we can start fresh. My girlfriend says men are like buses, another one'll be along in a minute. Not a dreamboat like Frank, I told her. He cannot be topped. I am hoping for the best outcome."

Maylou shut her eyes. Her mama in Beulahland, Elvis in Graceland, herself nothing but a hound dog. Loss was as achy a thing as love. It was one of the factors that had brought all these people together, mourning Elvis, but other losses too. Some so tiny and peculiar there was no explaining them.

"Cockapoos are not as pretty as they used to be," the woman went on. "That's a known fact. I would like to get a pup cute as a bug's ear. Imagine Elvis adoring peacocks and Dean Martin also. He was a man with definite preferences—did you read *Elvis and Me*? A cockapoo would keep me company nights when Frank works late. I hate to eat alone, it's bourgeois. He thinks I'm bowling. Years ago Frank's passion could melt the stars. When I look at him I see a little boy."

"I don't know about love," Maylou said. "Is it true that love never dies? How do you pick the right people to love?"

"Nobody's an expert, least of all me. I would say—love yourself, love Elvis, then be very selective. Get real proof of it, nothing circumstantial or hearsay. Don't love with your heart, love with your head. And at the beginning, don't go overboard buying gifts."

They sat thinking about this for a moment and then the woman got up. "I heard Elvis liked pork rinds," she said. "So that's what I brought. I don't know if that's thoughtful or dumb."

"I brought the lid off a cookie jar," Maylou said, since it'd been getting on her nerves rattling. "And a pocketful of dreams," she added. "A million-dollar smile, besides."

"Smile though your heart is breaking," the woman said. "Smile and the whole world smiles with you. That's the truth. My gran used to tell me I was destined for greatness, we'll have to wait and see. Wish me luck, with Frank, I mean. Keep a spiritual journal and every day find something uplifting to write down, even if it seems trivial. We're all stuck with our own dark shadows. Set your sights on a distant star. There was only one Harry Houdini, escape for the rest of us isn't such a neat trick."

Maylou found a hotel at the end of Lonely Street and settled in for the night. She'd be home tomorrow and couldn't guess what lay around the corner. She figured she'd unpack, then tuck her mama into the Gates of Heaven cemetery for the longest sleep of all. Eternity. Her mama had passed.

Things kept coming back to Maylou, like her mama holding a bottle of Windex and a paper towel, wiping off the bathroom mirror. "Honey, I know puberty is difficult," she'd say, "but if you want to practice French kissing do it on your palm. There are lip smears all over my mirrors. A boy can take it but it's wearing me out. Nice girls find other forms of expression."

Maylou had a slice of while-u-wait pizza for dinner. She flipped through different channels on the TV and took a bath. She looked at herself for a long time in the fogged mirror. She didn't mind her appearance since she was a believer in beauty being not only skin deep, which gave her an out on so-so days. Plus, she'd been told she was nothing to sneeze at and didn't doubt it. Men were never on the debit side. Maylou had turned to them for fondling whenever she found herself eclipsed by the sun. Didn't seem they could ever swell her heart for long, though—Zak her spouse most especially. Maylou glanced over at her mama's letter propped against the bedside lamp still waiting to be read. Her mama had been her haven in a blizzard. Maylou held the envelope up to the light and saw the letter silhouetted inside.

She remembered worrying nights and nights as a child about her mama dying. It was a consideration, her mama being forty-two when Maylou was less than a minute old. That was the only gap between them and it troubled her.

When Wylie, her best friend grades one through four, would ask her who she would save first, her mother or her father, if there was an uncontrollable fire and she could carry only one parent on her back to safety before the whole place went up in smoke, who would it be? Maylou had never hesitated in picking her mama. There was no guilt involved. Her father gave her what she needed, but she didn't know anything about him as a who's who. She couldn't possibly have made a list of his likes and dislikes, for example. She wasn't even sure which column she'd fall into herself.

She knew with crystal clarity though that she was the apple of her mama's eye and would fill pages of a "like" list. Her mama showered love without being drippy. "Love is not proud," she'd say. "I waited twenty years for you, you can't imagine the time, and finally many nights of real love with your daddy brought you about. As an adult, I want you to be happy and independent, maybe an architect. Someone who can make up her own mind and keep her house neat and tidy. I was once a little girl myself and have no illusions, though I have fond wishes. I hope your future will be prosperous to say the least."

Maylou turned the envelope over, smoothed her finger across her name written on the front. She knew she had to take hold of her life. She couldn't waft like a dandelion puff on air. All the blurry faces, strangers and family had to come into focus. Her daddy was no help, out there in the woods speaking in tongues, but at least he'd found a faith depository. CeCe was going to write to the producers of *That's Incredible!* and tell them about his Forest of Enlightenment. She was going to mention Sherman as an interesting sidebar, using his formal stage name, drawing attention to his psychic abilities and chapbook. She was convinced a TV crew would be out in a flash to film the whole thing. The exposure might be just what the doctor ordered. Hordes of curiosity seekers would be dropping by at all hours of the day and night with crisp U.S. currency to unload. CeCe was already freezing batches of Rice Krispie squares so they'd have something to nibble on. She said this was just the kind of project she could sink her teeth into. Maybe she was looking at the world through rose-colored glasses, but it was about time she did.

Maylou got under the bedcovers, adjusted the lamp on the nightstand to shine directly onto her lap. It was now or never. She had no idea what to expect from her mama's letter. Maylou thought about Elvis leaving all the things he'd owned preserved at Graceland for tourists to come in and look at. Everybody left traces of themselves behind in the world when they died. Her mama had left clothes and jewelry and pills, and an envelope with Maylou's name on it tucked into the side compartment of a handbag Doris Morris had ended up with. Maylou breathed in deeply and unfolded the letter. For the first time she noticed how similar her mama's writing was to her own. She read:

"My darling Maylou,

If you are reading this correspondence it means that I am dead. What a thing. You were a precious gift and the joy of my life. I had a hunch all was not right with me though I couldn't put my finger on it. Was it my heart? I hate to leave you but after all you are a smart cookie in your middle twenties. I'm very proud of the way you turned out. We had some good conversations and a lot of laughs. I'm overlooking the tears though they were important too. Having you was the best thing I ever did. I think I was a good mama, I hope, and a good wife to your father. He loved me. You may not feel you know your daddy much but he is like that. Whistle and he'll be there, not like a dog but like a true-blue good man. Which he is. I considered leaving him a note as well, but though my death will be hard on him at first, he'll soon find something to occupy his time. He's always got to be doing something with his hands. He would have made an in-demand upholsterer. A letter would stand in the way of his recovery, I believe. I loved him classically, romantically as any Juliet. We were tactful on a daily basis. You are going to feel marooned and I'm sorry for that. Maybe we will have some otherworldly contact, but don't get your hopes up, I'll have to check it out. You won't be scared if I say hello as a ghost, will you? That would bother me. Looking back, I am proud of some of my accomplishments. For example, I once saved a boy from drowning. I got many A's in school. Well, I'm not going to list everything I've done, but the point is I feel okay about signing off, so you know. Honey, your mama loves you. I had a good time. This is not the kind of note that's easy to end, even if Doris is ringing the doorbell. That woman frazzles my nerves. She thinks everyone is her bosom buddy. She has a flair for the dramatic. When I open the door there she'll be just as short as ever. I must say I like Vern, though, still waters run deep. God, I hope I can remember all the relations' names when I get to heaven. Pray for name tags. I love you, doll."

Maylou's heart bent around the words like a tiny hand holding firm the one leading the way into the light, into the songs of angels.

In the morning Maylou called Zak to say she was homing in on him. A woman's voice answered the telephone. Maylou hung up and dialed again. The woman answered, "You just dialed the exact same number, cheesecake. You wanna try again?"

"Is the lady of the house available?" Maylou said in a quiet voice.

"This is she. And speak up, I can hardly hear a word you're saying."

"My name is Pam," Maylou said. "I'm selling something."

"Something? Something like what, Pam?"

"I have to have your name before I can make my sales pitch," Maylou said. "It's personalized to you."

"Shirl," the woman said. Zak had lied like a rug.

"So what are you selling?" Shirl said. "Time is money, money is time."

"Light bulbs, I guess," Maylou said.

"Are you a cripple?" Shirl was getting interested.

"I'm a person crippled by love," Maylou said. "My heart's been slam-dunked once too often."

"I know what you mean. This man whose house I'm in was but a hiccup in my checkered past. I was playing the field in Wichita and having a ball. I was trying to put my finger on the source of my libido, paying close attention to any primal urges I might have. The id is a big mystery to me.

Then I got a message on my machine saying he was sick as a junkyard dog and couldn't get out of bed even to prepare a meal or wash. Thinking he might have mononucleosis, I rushed right over. My cousin had mononucleosis and couldn't do a thing to help herself. Lost all the weight she'd been storing since she was a baby. All she could do was lie there and stare at the ceiling. I bought her a remote control for the TV but she was afraid to use it. I think she thought it was a laser beam. Turns out there's nothing the matter with this guy a roll in the hay won't fix and that's what he's got on his mind. He took my car keys and hid them. I'm a virtual prisoner of my trusting nature. I feel a nervous break-down coming on. All I want to do is eat finger sandwiches, is that normal? I'm climbing the walls."

"May I make a suggestion?" Maylou said.

"Be my guest."

"Check the flour bin in the breakfast nook for your keys," Maylou advised.

"Hang on." Shirl put the phone down. In a minute she was back. "Well, isn't that something. Pam, give me your address, I'd like to send you a nosegay. I'm an amateur flower arranger in my leisure time. Now, I can't say when it will arrive because leisure time is something that's eluding me. I'm attempting to cut back on my sleep in order to give myself more of it. I want to improve the quality of my life and leisure time is the way I see to do it. Leisure time is something we routinely neglect. No wonder we're all crying the blues. If we can get to the point where leisure time equals or surpasses work time, then we have a chance at happiness. I myself have not been truly happy for years. I used to think sex would do it but leisure time is the real key. Sex, on the other hand, is worthwhile; don't get me wrong. Sex is life-enforcing and power-bestowing, but it won't make you happy. Not in a million years. Only ample leisure time can guarantee happiness. Pam, I hope your life is chock-full of leisure time. I've always wanted to live in a lighthouse and now that I have my car keys back there's nothing to stop me. Lighthouses are chic."

"Follow your heart until you reach your dreams," Maylou said. "That's from a musical where a whole family walks across the Alps fleeing Nazis. They thought they had it made but the trip proved overly tiresome for the littler family members who could hardly keep up."

"In life it's always a matter of keeping up. I try to aim for autonomy of spirit," Shirl said. "March to your own drumbeat. That way you can go at a snail's pace and enjoy the peaceful moments. Euphoria is around the next bend anyway. You can see why I have no need for light bulbs. Electricity is a state of mind."

"Though we didn't clinch a deal, I'm glad I called from my forsaken outpost," Maylou said. "I'm at a crossroads. Home is where the heart is, but my heart is with a dead person. Where does that leave me?"

"Listen, poptart, love is like a boomerang. The harder you throw it away, the faster it comes back. Now that doesn't directly apply to your situation, but it's true nevertheless. You've got to pucker up and give life a smacker. Go on. Let grief knock you around the room a little and then decide what you want. I, for example, want to wake up every morning at the top of a lighthouse. Have a code to live by. I want to avoid cheapskates and wear pretty lace panties, for example. And you already know how I feel about leisure time. Do you see what I'm driving at, Pam?" Shirl paused. "Don't sweat the small stuff. At present you're a zombie, neither dead nor alive. You've got to drag the life in you to the surface, rely more on your id. Ride a white horse bareback into a tangled wood, if you get my drift. Pam, nobody but you can make you happy. Be sassy and throw caution to the wind. I get the feeling this dead person has sent you into a tailspin."

"I agree that I'm a tempest in a teapot," Maylou said. "I want what I can't have. The other options seem unremarkable."

"The other options are all you've got, cupcake. Leisure time is too fleeting to spend it dwelling on impossibilities and the never-never. Death narrows the scope, I admit. But tell me what it is you want and we'll take it from there." Shirl felt plain Episcopalian.

"I want a direction. Someone trustworthy to love, and a job I can get ahead at. Also I want a chance to say goodbye," Maylou said. "More than anything I want that. A fond farewell."

"Okay, but on a smaller scale, I meant. Like do you want to live in a lighthouse or buy a new outfit? Your goals are too big is your problem. Recovery starts with being happy about the teeniest things. I want you to be myopic, Pam. Enjoy a nice hot cup of coffee, take a dog for a walk. Cool your jets on the love scene, the idea is to keep yourself intact. A cowboy rides into the picture trying to corral your heart, you throw mud in his eye."

"My other line is ringing," Maylou said. "I better go."

"I enjoyed our tete-a-tete. If it was smoke detectors you were selling we might've done business. You can't be too careful where fire is concerned. My brother, the pyromaniac, used to set little fires around the neighborhood and now I have a self-contained phobia," Shirl said. "There are many kinds of scars as you know, first and second degree. I like your soft-sell approach, Pam. I'm off to the coast to find a suitable lighthouse. I foresee good things so long as I don't get mixed up with drug runners."

"Bye for now then," Maylou said and hung up. So that was Shirl. Maylou looked at the phone. They were ships passing in the night, strangers on terra firma.

Tucked behind the phone where some previous occupant had left it, Maylou saw a lone seashell. She guessed she wasn't the only fish in the sea driving cross-country. Probably hotels around the south were littered with shells gathered meditatively, taken from the shore for some purpose forgotten by checkout time. Maylou held the shell to her ear and heard her mama singing in it.

Fourteen

MAYLOU WAS ON HER WAY BACK. She drove at a
constant speed, with a constant expression on her face. She
passed more than a few eighteen-wheelers with naked ladies
reclining on their mud flaps. The original mud wrestlers,
she thought.

She passed a bad accident where a man was being loaded
into an ambulance. The man's car was a disaster and Maylou
could see the circular hole in the windshield where the man's
head had pushed through. There was no other car around,
no probable cause. She imagined the man had been on his
way to meet a new lover. The lover had waited smoking
cigarettes, staring at her watch. Every now and then she had
checked her lipstick in the mirror, smoothed her silky hair.
Finally, the lover had decided the man was not going to
show and she'd closed the door to the motel and driven her
car away. At her apartment, she'd packed her clothes into
suitcases and left the town for good. She knew that she was
so ugly she was unworthy of love, of even an afternoon's
pleasure. As the man's head hit the glass he'd thought, now
she will never know how beautiful she is.

Maylou drove through a small town where a white frame
house was on fire. The flames rose thirty feet in the air and

the smoke was gray and black and yellow. Volunteer firemen were running from all directions pulling their coveralls up over their regular clothes. Next to the white house was a pretty yellow one and soon smoke was rippling off its roof too. Then flames were shooting out from under its shingles. The black woman who owned the pretty yellow house stood in front crying. Across the street, two old white sisters were on their porch with their arms around one another, their faces full of pity. He's got the whole world in His hands. You and me, sister.

By now nothing much was left of the white frame house and the volunteer firemen went to work on the yellow. They shot so much water onto the roof of the yellow house that shingles came off in chunks and fell to the grass below. The black woman was busy running into and out of her little burning house carrying lamps and cushions and all her things and placing them on the grass in a pile. The things looked shabby and unrelated, inspected out of context by the crowd that had gathered to watch the fire burn down her house.

Big black men left their places in the crowd and walked into the kindled home for the first time. They came out carrying sofas and tables and a brand new Sony TV. The woman directed the big men where on the lawn she wanted each thing put, like she was decorating a new room, which she was. The carpet was plush and the ceiling was sky blue.

Maylou passed a long-forgotten graveyard with crooked tombstones barely rising above the earth. The boneyard was set next to a boarded-up gas station which had been indicated by a sign on the highway as a place open for business. There was nothing else around. Maylou pulled into the deserted gas station since the door to the Ladies was swinging open and she had a need. The washroom was spanking clean with a new bar of soap, a full roll of toilet paper, and a shiny steel-rimmed mirror above the sink. Maylou found all this convenient, but odd.

She lingered in the washroom, knowing she was being a pokey Moses getting home, but who could blame her. Life was offering her crumbs when she wanted the whole strudel. True, nobody had promised her a rose garden but anybody looking could see she was being lambasted by an ill wind. Her mama bygone, her daddy out of retirement in the woods beyond Arkadelphia. She was feeling in the mood to give her husband a knuckle sandwich, which he deserved, but she felt too blank to care. Zak was somebody she used to love a lot and there was something about having felt that way once that made it tough not to feel that way anymore. Shirl answering the phone was too many straws for the camel, but. Adultery of an incurable strain was hard to immunize against.

Maylou watched a daddy-longlegs make its way across the wall of the washroom. It put to mind Long Dong Silver's proportions. Proved her theory that anything with overextended parts in one area had to trade off with extra small parts in others. Like Long Dong's minuscule teeth compared to his famed namesake part, and the spider's puny body compared to its elegant Ginger Rogers legs. Maylou wondered what kind of courage it took oddballs like them, and others she'd seen, to get through the nights of doubt and self-incrimination they had to have. Extra-pretty people and ugly people, both, wrestled with beauty esteem. Joe Averages just figured they were acceptable door prizes the way they were. Better to be plain than stupid, her mama always said.

When Maylou finally came out of the washroom, she saw an old man with a mop peering into her station wagon. His immaculate Pinto was parked alongside. The man's bald head was set atop a skinny neck and he moved the head up and down, side to side, like a periscope looking in the window.

"Hey you," Maylou called. "Beside that Pinto."

The man spun around. "I'm on the up-and-up," he yelled.

Maylou met the man halfway. "I came to spruce up the John," he said, waving the mop. "There's not usually anyone here but me these days. Looks like you've been on a trip, couldn't help but notice the Kansas plates. Only thing I know about Kansas, even though we're close, is the Wizard of Oz, that girl Dorothy and her dog Toto. Cute dog, seemed smart and helpful too. My wife and I, she's dead, used to watch that movie every year around Easter when it came on. She loved the munchkins. Ivy, I still like the sound of my wife's name after all this time—the sound of a whisper in bed—she knew a munchkin female personally. The little gal said that movie was the hardest work she ever had to do. The hours were long and the director treated them with harsh words, maybe thinking they were as short on feelings as they were on height, which of course is not true. They had to sing that song, 'Ding dong, the witch is dead,' until they were hoarse in the throat. Turned out quite a memorable number, though you don't like to think of those poor munchkins with sore vocal chords as a result, especially when the song is one of great relief and rejoicing that the witch is dead. Judy Garland often ate lunch with the munchkins, who were not debauched drunks, and signed their autograph books when-ever they asked. Miss Garland treated them like they were movie stars in their own right. Her daughter, Liza, is not such a lady from what I hear. Ivy used to keep on top of the star gossip. The sicker she got with her cancer, the more impor-tant the stars' personal lives became. You see, Ivy'd always fancied herself a would-be starlet, she had beautiful hair.

'Somewhere over the rainbow skies are blue. There, all the dreams that you dare to dream really do come true.' And 'there's no place like home, there's no place like home'— some memorable lines were in that movie. Seems like you're almost home yourself." The man had limpid eyes.

"Home," Maylou said, "is sweet but elusive. Not as easy a place to get to as you'd think. My journey has been more than a ride down a road. My mama died in Florida and I'm trying to make my way back." Maylou felt like she'd been gone a long time, an unreal amount of time as in a play where a lot happens in two hours. Whole lives are lived. Maylou's world seemed a kind of staged reality. She kept waiting for her mama to come from the wings and take the spotlight. She wanted to finish the play like they'd rehearsed. The curtain would fall only when they'd both said all their lines, everything that needed to be said.

"The way back," the man said, "is always harder than the way there, which is ofttimes a breeze. Until Ivy comes for to carry me home, I plan to keep this Ladies room a welcome oasis to female travelers like yourself. I ran this filling station once and the compliments I got were not on the service, which was fast and friendly, but on the nice clean Ladies room. On the road, men like a chance to piss on the soft shoulder. This is not the case for women. They like a washroom on the road to be as sanitary and welcoming as their own at home. Ivy taught me that, and she was right too. If you believe in reincarnation you'd know that Ivy had been here before. Her instincts were bang-on. Though life for her was never a picnic, it was no mystery either. She always had a sensible answer to my questions. I had a lot of questions over the years. Ivy'll be born again. Whenever I see a little baby I look it right in the eyes hoping to see her looking back at me. Maybe if you look at enough babies, your mama will look out at you from one of them. It's a hopeful thing. Anybody who's had somebody die on them knows what it is to look a baby square in the eye."

"When I get home," Maylou said, "there's a tea room I know of where I'm going to try to contact my mama through ESP. Red Dog'll hook me up for a price. It's worth the effort. I've got questions of my own, though I can't find words for them. My mama might be able to guess."

"If peacocks can fly, anything's possible, is what Ivy would say. And she'd be right. If you made up the weirdest thing you could think of, the real world would already have something weirder to show. There's no need for an imagination in the U.S.A."

Maylou smiled, she was feeling outwardly sociable.

"I better get on with my bathroom," the man said then. "I can't wait to get home. I'm working my way page by page through a new fondue cookbook. I enjoy a good fondue."

As Maylou was backing out in the station wagon the old man came running towards her, waving for her to wait a minute. He dug around the back of his shiny Pinto and then came over.

"Here's a little something," he said, "to add sparkle." He passed Maylou a jar of Turtle wax. "With my compliments. I always find the more luster there is in general, the better I feel."

Maylou was pleased. "You know," she said, "I'm in no special hurry to get home. I wouldn't mind giving you a hand stirring that fondue. If you'd want."

"Sure," the man said. "You're on. My bathroom chores can keep till tomorrow, I guess. Bob's Special Fondue takes priority."

"Is Bob your name?" Maylou asked.

"Bob? No," the man said. "Bob's Special Fondue is where I'm up to in the cookbook. I guess it was some Bob thought up the particular recipe we're attempting to duplicate."

"My name's Maylou P., for Puce, Turner," Maylou said. "Pleased to meet you."

"It would be nice to be on a first-name basis over our meal," Maylou tried another way. "I would like to know your name so I'll refer to you correctly if I ask you to pass something."

"Oh, fine. Errol Flynn Jr.," the man said. "The junior and the rest is a coincidence to the star of the silver screen. My daddy was Errol Flynn Sr. but not the actor. I don't believe he used a Sr. in his name, or a Jr. either. That would be a real fluke."

Maylou got into Errol's perfect Pinto and they sped away as the sun went down, dragging her ruby nails soft across the sky's blue back. She could still feel the heat.

"My wife Ivy always wanted a horse," Errol said, "but it was never to be. After she went to Her Reward, I bought this car with a horse's name and hoped she might think that was a good one. Ivy and I shared a lot of chuckles over the years. I'm a light sleeper by nature, and one thing I remember fondly is the way she would sometimes roll over in bed at night and wake herself up. She'd open her eyes for a second, see me looking at her, and smile. Then she would close her eyes and be asleep again in no time. But she would smile first. It always seemed to me that a smile that came easy as that in the middle of the night was worth something. A smile like that was a kiss. Ivy was a person knew how to make you feel good without trying. She would have made a great mother."

"You never had offspring?" Maylou said.

"We had one baby. I delivered it myself back when we were still on the farm. It was a little boy but there was something wrong with him. He was born with his head full of water. Ivy never put him down. For two weeks straight she carried him everywhere she went and sang him songs and told him what all she was doing. Then one night he just died in his sleep with his little face nestled into her armpit. Ivy buried him herself out in the orchard so that the cycle of her creation would be complete. She thought our boy was born knowing the sadness of the world and so his head came full of tears. Ivy was remarkably insightful. I hear nowadays they save babies like him as a matter of course. Progress is a great thing if you're on the platform to meet it."

Errol's house was a neat-as-a-pin bungalow poised behind a rambling Mock Orange hedge.

"You'll see Ivy's touches throughout," he said, opening the front door. "People have said her personality is reflected in the decorating. She had a nice personality for a southpaw. She would have thought a fondue fun."

Errol went to work in the kitchen and wouldn't let Maylou do a thing to help. He told her why didn't she go take a bubble bath and relax until dinner was ready. He said she could help herself to towels and the clean bathrobe hanging on the door. Errol wanted her to be at home where he lived.

While the bath water was running, Maylou opened and closed drawers and cupboards quietly. Everything was in perfect order except for the bottom drawer in the vanity, which must have been Ivy's. The drawer was packed with beauty paraphernalia: eye shadows, lipsticks, blushes, nail polish, powder—all in varying shades of coral and all jumbled together. Maylou burrowed through the makeup like it was a discount bin at the drugstore. A messy drawer was irresistible in the way a pristine drawer never could be. She picked out a bottle of nail polish and painted her toenails

Peach Melba. Then she coated her lips Coral Gables. She dropped a shiny orange bath oil bead into the tub of water and got in after twisting her black hair into a knot. Maybe she'd just live on here eating fondues and taking baths.

Without her mama Maylou could pretty much do anything she pleased. There was the swelling notion of freedom in her thoughts, the yen to keep on driving and never deal with Zak again, keep her heart to herself. The freedom was sad though. It was the kind of unasked-for release orphans knew, and those dumped from love. It was freedom gained through loss, and that given a choice few would have chosen. Most would rather be tied down to a loving relationship because then the strings attached were of so fine a silk, so steely strong a thread, that the web they created was perfect, a fortress rather than a trap. It was a place to go away from and come back to, that rightly called itself home.

An hour later Maylou was fast asleep in the tub when a rock landed in the water beside her. The rock had a toothy, boyish face painted on it which she saw as she lifted it from the water. A note was attached and Maylou read, GRUB'S UP, before the blurring ink took over. The note seemed cheerful and spur-of-the-moment, the rock face dandy, and Maylou filled with a heap of joy towards the world. She put on the terry bathrobe and met Errol in the dinette. The fondue pot was in the middle of the table and smelled delicious. She let her hair down.

"There you are," Errol said. "My pacemaker went loopy to think of you drowned in my tub. That wouldn't look good. I knocked first, but I guess you didn't hear me. I thought I'd better take measures. My niece sent me that pet rock for my birthday." Errol stirred the fondue which sent the smell recirculating around the room. "Bob sure knew what he was doing with this fondue. He was a maestro to cheese, the way Liberace was to the piano. We're in for a treat."

"I have to confess I borrowed Ivy's nail polish for my niggly toes," Maylou said. She put the pet rock on the table. "You don't mind, I thought."

"I don't mind. Ivy loved peach, you may have noticed the preponderance. A very feminine color. Ivy was wearing peach when we wedded and her appreciation of the color never waned. Her casket was lined with peach satin which the undertaker thought was an extravagance, as though I cared what he thought."

"Sounds like you and Ivy had an understanding. I think she would have considered herself smiled upon," Maylou said.

"We had a mutual admiration society going. In life's marathon we ran neck-in-neck. To my way of thinking, Ivy herself was peachy."

For a while they made short work of the fondue. Then Errol said, "Maylou, an old man like me can't help preaching when he sees an opening to do it. You seem a private person and it brings to mind a sponge. Everybody wants an ear to shout into. When you come along with those big eyes that have seen sadness, people want to spill their beans. It's all very well to absorb, but you have to wring yourself out too. People can do a lot of talking without saying a single thing and you don't want to squander your time. I don't expect to be your ear since we're not blood brothers, or kissing cousins, but there are people out there who will help you if you call their names. Having somebody you love die makes all the world seem cold and indifferent, but that's not the case. The heart never takes pain lying down. It swells to a lump in your throat that prevents you talking even if you wanted to. Ivy taught me how to be jubilant and let my heart soar. She was a knower-of-ropes."

Maylou said, "My mama too. I miss her smarts."

And Errol Flynn Jr. winked like they were in on something together, before he brought out dessert. Little stale cakes were served with fresh coffee. Maylou admired an extensive thimble collection that hung on the wall in a hardwood showcase.

"In fact," Errol said, "I just received today in the mail my brand new Advertising Art of Yesteryear thimble. The series of twelve celebrates the famous trademarks of yesteryear that captured the imagination of millions and made them want to buy the products. I already have Elsie the Cow, the yellow Bon Ami chick, and Hills Bros.' ancient coffee taster. They're solid pewter and hand-painted. Today I got the Morton Salt thimble. It has the charming girl with the umbrella that made Morton Salt a household name when it came out in 1914. Inside I had to use my magnifying glass, but the slogan 'Morton Salt—When it Rains it Pours' is written. Very clever. They send one every month, but the one I can't wait to get is the Dutch Boy, I hear there are tiny bristles in his paint brush. They threw in Sir Thomas Lipton for those who sent away the first. I have one hundred and fifty-two thimbles."

"I admire that stick-to-itness," Maylou said.

"Ivy was never a collector. She liked arts and crafts but there's nothing to show for it. She took a course in macrame but gave her tangle of knots to Mel and his plain wife Babe for Christmas."

"I never did macrame," Maylou said. "I want to learn waterpainting. You can make some dreamy things all running around together."

"Ivy took that. Getting back to my thimbles," Errol said, "if you're ever anywhere, you could buy me one for my collection. From Kansas, America's Heartland, with a munchkin on it or the ruby slippers. Weren't they something? Click, click and you were safe in bed. You put to mind Dorothy but for want of a little pooch."

"I had a wiener dog old as the hills," Maylou said. "He's in a foster home now with a boy made a whoop-de-do over him and there he longed to remain. I think chemistry happens between living beings and it's best not to tamper with it."

"Ivy was a magnet," Errol said. "She loved to try food bites in the supermarket and swim."

Maylou offered to load the dishwasher but Errol wouldn't hear of it.

"I'll just wash our few things in Palmolive like I always do," he said. "Thanks though."

Later he played to her on his ukulele and gave her a glass of warm milk to drink. Maylou tucked down on the daybed in the conversation area. Sometime deep within the night, she awoke from the dreams she was daring to dream. Errol Flynn Jr. crooned, "Where troubles melt like lemon drops that's where you'll find me. If pretty little bluebirds fly over the rainbow, why then oh why can't I?"

In the morning the clouds were far behind them and Errol drove Maylou back to the gas station for her car.

"Tiptoe through life's tulips with nary a second thought," he said. "Be light as air and truly mean well."

Maylou complimented the thimbles, fondue and ukulele. "In the future I want to say I'm fine, and leave it at that," she said. "I want to give more than I get and be remembered as nice."

"You would have loved Ivy," Errol said. "Boy, was she nice. Though she was good at things, her head stayed small and self-contained and there's too few people you can say that about. Ivy would have wanted you to know that a like-it-or-lump-it policy doesn't hold water. Be all that you can be, and don't be waylaid by silly whims. She was my bridge over troubled water and not a day goes by that I don't miss her."

"There's nothing halfway about love," Maylou said. "I'll long remember Ivy and her passion for peach and your passion for her."

"She was a born leader, tomorrows were always good with Ivy. I'm all for tomorrow," Errol said.

"I used to look forward to things and be a trooper," Maylou said. "But I guess you haven't failed to notice that I am not myself."

"No one is themself entirely, we are all bits and pieces of everyone else. We're part people who we want to be, and part people who we don't want to be, but are anyway. Everybody is everybody else to some degree. That's why we say we don't know who we are. That's why we say we want to find ourselves. And that's how you can like or not like someone when you've just met them, because you quicken to a thing behind their eyes. You might as well know, the only way to find yourself as somebody separate is to be in love. Then when you are alone you know it. That's why you miss your mama and I miss Ivy. They were part of what makes us us, and now they're gone, we're not sure if the leftovers are going to be enough to get by on. It's like having but the one kidney."

"I knew somebody with one kidney," Maylou said. "He made do with minor sacrifices. For example he had to forgo his jujitsu, since his opponents would have been obliged to kick him in the remaining kidney and thus end his life."

"Self-defense is the only sport in which low blows are tolerated if not admired," Errol said. "Those black belts are cunning, have vaulted IQ's, and snappy little hands and feet. They bow in an ancient but friendly way. Often they grow bonsai trees in their spare moments, pinching the roots with steely determination and their quick little fingers."

At the gas station Maylou thought she'd use the Ladies before she hit the dusty trail. Someone had been in there during the night and written on the wall, littered toilet paper and two Sweet Marie wrappers on the floor.

"Someone made a pit stop during the night," she said to Errol when she came out. "You can read the writing on the wall."

"Yes," Errol said, "the sign on the highway still draws them. But that's what makes my job rewarding. So far, mostly people just leave their names and the date. Like a diary, I suppose they think, or a guest registry. Once there was even an Ivy. She used a small "i" instead of a big one and the dot over it was a fat heart. I thought maybe that Ivy was fat herself, maybe a soft friend to a shy boy. Usually Mr. Clean gets the writing off but I let that Ivy set where it was awhile."

"This writing is a note of sorts," Maylou said. "No name to speak of. I quote: 'I have an eating disorder. I binge and purge, binge and purge. I am on my way to get help. Help.'"

"A washroom is not a confessional," Errol said. "I have my work cut out for me. I don't get paid under the table for my trouble. I use honest elbow grease."

Before she left Maylou kissed Errol Flynn Jr. full on the mouth. As she backed away in the wagon, she saw him looking in the Ladies room mirror. He licked the peach smear from his lips and Maylou wondered did he taste sweet the memory of Coral Gables, his wife's fruity kiss?

Fifteen

MAYLOU DROVE through the rounded hills and broad valleys of her home state whose motto was, "To the Stars Through Difficulty." She could not shake Dr. Brewster Higley's theme, "Home on the Range," which was orchestrating in her head. The skies above her stretched vast and blue, as though a bucket of paint had been spilled across. The grassy slopes hither and yon were sprinkled with summer wildflowers, asters, clover, sweet william, verbena. The lakes and streams brimmed, Maylou knew, with catfish, crappie, striper, gar. Around her the light was clear and bright, nature in its element was colorful and piquant. She imagined below the surface of the lakes' cold water, movement, hefty numbers of fish darting to and fro, safe in their murk until tempted to the delectable bait, the shiny lure of men.

Maylou stopped for lunch at a diner in Eudora that had a sign in the window advising a fried fish special and the coming of Indian Powwow Day. Plains Indians tribes of Cheyenne and Comanche would be coming out in traditional garb to eat barbeque and show handicrafts. Zak was some part Kickapoo. The Kickapoos, though late settlers to Kansas, were promised to turn out at the powwow in full feather. Maylou could imagine her husband riding a wild Appaloosa, waving a tomahawk, dancing naked for rain, showering squaw after squaw with his equal, flawed affection. "You are more beautiful than Hiawatha," he'd say time after time, kissing jojoba-slicked braids. "Wanna wrestle?"

Maylou sat down at the diner's counter. A waitress right away put a cup and saucer in the space in front of her, poured coffee not asking first if that's what Maylou wanted, not saying boo or hello. The waitress dropped two creams from her hand before walking the length of the counter filling cups the way along, all from the same pot. It was like being pecked on the cheek by an aunt you didn't much know, Maylou thought. Distant, but some care was given.

"How many cups you figure you go through in a day, Coralee?" a man at the end of the counter asked the wait-ress, as she poured what may have been his tenth by the ciga-rettes stubbed in the ashtray in front of him. The waitress rolled her eyes like it was too many to even think about, the way a true bottomless cup would be. She said, "I don't know. I just keep pouring it out and hope them in the bean depart-ment over in Colombia are keeping up with me."

Maylou was sitting beside a woman picking at her food and arguing under her breath. Maylou caught, "I'm not going to say that. I'm tired of being thought of as disturbed, Almon. I'll consume however much pie I feel like, you're in no position to censor me." The woman took a hunk of pie into her mouth. "Oh, all right," she hissed, chewing and swallowing some. She nudged Maylou with her elbow.

"Almon Purvis says hi," she said, reluctantly.

"Me?" Maylou checked around her. The woman's elbow was just leaving her side. "Not me," Maylou said.

"You," the woman said. "Almon Purvis says hi. I should know, I'm still his wife."

Coralee came over on hearing the talk. "Lynette," she said, addressing the pie-downing woman like she was an animal she didn't want to scare away, "how's that new huckleberry recipe? You know, Almon's been gone a good long time. What would he be doing hanging around saying hi to her for?" The waitress nodded towards Maylou in a way made Maylou think maybe she figured she couldn't speak out for herself.

"Almon says your mama's doing fine," Lynette said, still reluctantly. "She talks about you fondly in the always current moment they live in." She took another bite of her pie. "Oh for pity's sake, Almon. Leave me be," the woman mumbled to her late husband. "You act like it's baby puppies I'm eating instead of this nice wedge of pie. I think you're jealous."

Coralee shrugged and walked off. To make more coffee, Maylou supposed, to top everyone's up.

Maylou interrupted the woman's rant, taking herself by surprise meaning to pursue conversation. "Excuse me," she said. "My mama's gone over. You're barking up the wrong tree here."

"No," Lynette said, wiping her mouth with a napkin like she just knew she wasn't going to be let to eat in peace. "Almon says Flossie's worried you're taking it all too hard. She'd hoped her goodbye letter would've acted as more of a comfort than it did." The woman leaned into Maylou and her hair, sweet-smelling and hard as china, brushed Maylou's cheek. "There's no love like a mama's for her baby," she whispered. "It doesn't stop with the grave. It goes on and on because it was never natural to share a body and then be pulled apart. It makes more sense to lay an egg, then it's just something you sit on and fuss over every while. When another heart is beating inside you, next to your own, that's another matter. Something you'll never forget or take lightly.

My own kids have broken my heart so many times it still hurts. When you're pregnant you don't care what sex your baby will be, or any other details neither. You just want whatever it is out in the open, where you can see what you're dealing with and get your hands on it, smell its soft head. Almost from then, you love that baby like you could hardly stand it. They turn on you like Dobermans though, willy-nilly, and you don't know what you did to deserve it. You'll see what I mean one day."

Lynette stood up. She crossed to the door and then stopped and said for Maylou, "I just want to make it through. Nervous energy and previous commitments are what keep me going. The heart is a lonely hunter, it better get a move on or starve." Her dress, Maylou noticed, was on inside out. The woman's face clouded over, she was listening to her husband from the near beyond. "Almon wants me to pass something on, but I can hardly hear what he's saying. He was never one to enunciate. Speak up, Purvis," she said briskly. "My ears aren't the keen receptacles they once were."

Maylou turned slightly and caught herself in the mirror behind the counter. She was twisting her mama's gold chain around her neck. She thought she looked like she'd just been dropped into a neighborhood she didn't know, where the signs were in code and the people wouldn't stop to give her direction. She watched herself hold her cup out to the waitress who was sweeping past on her coffee route. She watched as her hand fumbled with the creamer, stirred the spoon shakily around the cup. She met her own eyes darkly over the brim as she took a long sip. Maylou thought how, if she were someone else seeing herself sitting there, she'd feel sorry. She might think about her in sad flashes the rest of the day and wonder what to make of it.

"Daughter," Lynette said, "is the most beautiful word." And she turned and walked out.

"Boy oh boy," Coralee said, when the door had closed. "Some people. Lynette's eldest was affianced to my Tulip, but he broke it off at the last second. Tulip had to be prescribed a series of mild tranquilizers that made her hair fall out. He went and eloped her off anyway when she was bald as a cub scout's butt. I got a postcard later saying she and Jerome were daytime friends and nighttime lovers. They both grew their hair long and yellow like the amber waves of grain from these parts Tulip missed. They're back in Leoti now, the Pinto Bean Capital."

"Love blinds with a strange light," Maylou said. "Unlike any other." She took a sip of coffee, feeling her heartbeat slow some. She'd heard her mama cutting the airwaves true as a knife. "Love hurts your eyes to look and requires a certain pooh-poohing of fear," Maylou added, somewhat mysteriously she even thought herself.

"Hm," the waitress came back with. "Tulip sent me a rubber plant last week and told me the baby's dropped. For all my worries, I don't let my personal life get in the way of my ability to wait on tables. I adhere to a code of overall excellence and daily yoga. The Sun Greeting is my key to stress-management. One thing I've learned is you don't find roses growing on stalks of clover. You don't find anything unless you go looking for it and hunt it down."

"That's deep," the man at the counter said, motioning for a refill.

Zak's new used Impala was not in the drive when Maylou pulled up. She could hear the Topeka Youth Wind Ensemble practicing next door in Lowanda's garage. Lowanda would shoot anyone a bird who complained about the sound. There was no way she'd close the garage door, she said, and make her musicians inhale car grease and tool dust. Anybody walking up her drive would be given the finger first, questioned later. Lowanda suffered from sciatica, which people thought gave her cause to be irritable and unwed. Her musical ear was loved in equal measure her foul mouth and flying finger were feared. Lowanda had night vision, eyes that probed the darkest reaches and put to music what it was she found there. The Youth Wind Ensemble, generally oblivious to her talent, made her life miserable and her back dully ache.

Maylou unpacked the car and carried her mama's urn in her arms over the threshold like a bride brought home cherished. She set her mama on the fireplace mantel in the living room. Then she searched through her bag for Mildred, the clay donkey, and put her on the mantel beside her mama's ashen bones. She sat down in the big armchair across from the fireplace and looked at the alabaster urn. The house was humming quietly like it was breathing deep in sleep. Maylou took the quiet into her.

It seemed so unreal that her mama could be in a container on the mantelpiece, too comic and sad. Maylou thought how her mama'd bought the periwinkle trailer in Florida, fixed it up down to the petunias. She thought of her writing a letter to say, though she was dead, she loved her daughter still and it was all right. She thought of Doris walking around some mall in her mama's shoes. Maylou could picture clearly her mama's face in so many different moods—pride, pain, joy. Maylou knew the shapes her mama's face took in expressing her feelings, same as they were her own. Seemed, in thinking about her mama, it was all these moody faces Maylou recalled rather than any one poignant episode or other. She wondered if that was unusual, if she'd be hit by sound memories later.

She felt some panic looking around the room. Somehow being back in her own house let things sink in, the way traveling on the road and keeping moving hadn't. At home, Maylou thought, you could tell exactly what you had and exactly what you didn't have. If you took a chair out from the room you were in, you'd notice the empty space where it had been. If you took your mama from sitting on the chair, and put her sealed into an urn on the mantelpiece, you'd sure notice that. You'd see the telephone on the table that would never ring again with your mama on the other end. You'd see it like it was a science lesson: the difference between empty and full, having and wanting to have.

On the mantel, Mildred stood there lopsided, clumpy in peculiar places and Maylou couldn't take her eyes from it, like she was a camera zooming in. The statue was all she had to show the bond with her mama. Maylou hadn't thought about the donkey for years, hadn't even liked it for longer, and now she was putting all kinds of import on the thing because her mama had kept it and seen something cherishable in it. The mule seemed so heavy-laden with her mama's affection, and her own wishful thinking, that it bulged in every wrong place. It seemed to Maylou to symbolize the clumsy love she'd offered her mama, which had been willingly accepted as though it was some perfect treasure held out. It shamed Maylou that she hadn't done better lovewise for her mama. She crossed the room, lifted the clay figurine from the mantel and dropped it to the hardwood floor. It made a sharp clatter as it hit and broke, and then the house was quiet. Except for the noise.

Maylou thought, someone's been hurt. Who's crying? And then she realized it was she herself crying, a remote, sad wail which told of loss and love, and the start of a new life.

Maylou took deep breath after breath, each feeling like it was her first after years of not being able to move a muscle, of not using her full lungs.

She went into the kitchen for a glass of water and a dust-pan. For glue too, because on second thought neither Mildred nor love was perfect. There was a note from Zak on the Frigidaire. "M.—Have gone to Norton to bag some pheasant. Thought you'd be back sooner. While in Norton I'm going to visit the Presidential Also Ran Gallery and Doll Collection. Jimmie Ray told me about it, it's a gallery of paintings and biographies of presidential candidates who never got anywhere. Be back Thursday. P.S. There's no food and laundry."

Maylou would have liked to have seen Zak at that moment, the soft filter gone. She had a cloak of resolve about her, an eye to cleaning up mess. Scat, she would have told him. Shoo.

That night there was a full moon and Maylou stood out under it. Mildred was glued abstractly back together, seeming less burdened so. Next door, Lowanda was lit in the window, playing a flute in her slip. Her gray hair fell around her shoulders and she swayed her upper body like she was the musical notes wafting through air. At the end of her solo she bowed her head to a made-up audience, put her hand to her mouth, taken off guard by the standing ovation, and bowed again from the waist. Her sciatica triggered, she straightened with difficulty and spit her one and only dream onto the floor.

Sixteen

THE SUN SHONE its bouncy yellow light into the kitchen, setting glow to the Instant Breakfast Maylou was drinking while she went through the want ads. She needed a job, since Zak's money was something she didn't want to live off, any more than he was somebody she wanted to live with. She knew she didn't want to wait, type, clean, or mind babies. She did want to move up the ladder into a VIP's shoes. She wanted to wedge a corporate gap.

The Beauti-Fuller ad struck a harmonious chord with her. Maylou was bright, creative and had no necessary experience. She liked the idea of a negotiable salary and a health plan. She agreed that big was beautiful, in small doses. They told her to come right over and speak to the supervisor.

Maylou downed the rest of her liquid breakfast, and two bowls of Zak's Froot Loops for extra energy and the child-like pizzazz he swore it gave him. She showered, dressed for success, and was off for her interview, hoping to return employed by a heavy woman and brimming with newfound independence. The Beauti-Fuller head office was set above the stores in the local mall where there was also a major outlet of the Beauti-Fuller chain.

The office was overtly pretty. Mauve and aqua walls were looped with floral stencils, Frank Sinatra lulled smooth on tape. Maylou announced herself to a roly-poly secretary and sat down in a skirted chair. Soon she was called into the inner office of Supervisor Madge Weems.

Madge gave Maylou the once-over.

"To be blunt, we're a store for fat women," she said. "Let me qualify—we're a store for proud, overweight women. Women who have come to accept themselves for what they are, no more no less. They want to look fashionable and up-to-date, but may find it difficult to shop in the regular outlets. We believe big is better, though weight loss is encouraged for health reasons, and we offer Weight Watchers discount coupons with purchases of over one hundred dollars for those customers who want them. You fall short of hefty, so the employee discount would be of no use unless you're willing to do alterations, or have an overweight sister. The discount is only for you and your immediate family members' use. It's twenty percent the first year, thirty percent then on. The words fat, walloping, blubber are no-no's across our chain. I used the word fat earlier to set the scene for you. It was rash, I'm tired. The job is an office-bound position but still we make a point of hiring over-size women who are extremely capable, though often looked over elsewhere. On the chance that you may be seen as an inspiration, let's proceed. Have you ever written advertising copy?"

"No," Maylou said. "But I know what you mean by it."

"That's the job. We need a creative person to write compelling promotional copy for our print ads in catalogues, magazines, newspapers, flyers, etc. Nothing too fancy, we're not looking for a poet, just something that will get people's attention and make them think Beauti-Fuller would be a good place to shop. Easy, right?" Madge Weems had a phony smile and Maylou wondered if she thought she was fooling anybody with it. She made a point of not reciprocating her own face.

"I could try," Maylou said.

"Yes, well. Try," Madge said. "What's your sign?"

"Scorpio," Maylou said. "I'm perched on the cusp."

"That's something. You and I are astrologically compatible. Everybody carries a different set of luggage through life, perhaps ours will be made by the same manufacturer. Do you suppose you could think full-figured eight hours a day and still feel like yourself?"

Going by Madge's darting eyebrow, Maylou got the idea this was a trick question.

"I don't think I'd have to think full-figured to write appropriate ads. I may be slim picking but I have a broad and savvy air. I catch on. I believe I'm meant to do something in this life. I want people to look at me and say, she's sharp. I have something to offer. I like the idea of getting money for making things up."

"Well, this job will bore you eventually," Madge said. "You will end up considering yourself a salesman of sorts, which you won't like. Advertising creates people who think they're being friendly. My smile has lost its charm, it no longer opens doors. That's a very real danger. You don't want to always be climbing in through basement windows."

"No, in fact I don't," Maylou agreed.

"All right, I'm going to show you an illustration and I want you to write the copy for it. Natural flair will either jump out or not, as fate and talent would have it. As a rule you would work hand in hand with the illustrator or photographer from the start, but this is just to see. I want to stress that the Beauti-Fuller group frowns upon Wyatt Earps. We respect authority and believe in the attainment of goals through the efforts of the team. Outlaws are weeded diligently from our bed of flowers. To make it in advertising you must know the market, speak up, and let go of old grudges. Can you speak up?" Madge was hep to Maylou's quiet natural tendency.

"I have been nearly drowned by sadness of late," Maylou said, "but I am learning that the world has people in it who only seem strange. A shoulder to lay your head upon is just a stone's throw distant. Speaking up is what I most yearn to do. I've been left with only my own voice for company and I'm getting to like the sound of it, though I fear I'm telling myself to get out of the marriage I'm in. The more I listen, the more bones I have to pick."

"Yes," Madge said, handing Maylou a drawing of a large woman drinking champagne on a yacht. A portly man was standing nearby offering roses. Madge gave Maylou a pen and paper. "Fifty words max." she said. "New spring line." Then she began a series of chatty phone calls.

Maylou looked deep into the woman-on-the-yacht's eyes, studied her champagne-glossed lips. She tried to imagine how the woman felt, what it was she was hoping to get from the man, and what it was she was hoping to give him. Maylou couldn't recall a single other ad from anywhere as a guide. She figured since they'd gone to the trouble of putting the woman on a yacht, lifestyle was important. She figured Beauti-Fuller was selling the whole shooting match—the man, the roses, the boat, the champagne and not just the pantsuit the woman was wearing. The glint in her eyes was the product, and that was what Maylou tried to sell. She got the idea of advertising as a kind of religion. It made promises, urged faith, had a wide audience and took up a collection. She was about to be ordained and immediately felt the responsibility, the guilt and the giddy power embrace.

Madge read the copy. Maylou already couldn't remember what she'd written, but the woman's eyes and wet lips were still clear in her mind. Maylou thought the woman had resolved to break with the past and start fresh. Her sad times were over and what her parted lips were whispering was, anchors away.

"This is worthy of a small hoopla," Madge said. "This shines like a diamond mine."

"I tried to put my finger on the pulse," Maylou said.

"You did. There is more than an iota of flair here. Once I show this to the other supervisors, I believe the Beauti-Fuller chain will be pleased to offer you a starting position in our advertising department. I will let you know in a week by telephone."

"The world is my oyster," Maylou said, flashing her pearly whites.

Back home she called CeCe to check in on her daddy's current state of being.

"What now?" CeCe snapped into the phone on impact.

"CeCe?" Maylou's pearly outlook nosedived.

"Thank God it's you and not Doris. She's driving me crazy. You have no idea. She's tormenting that poor woman whose car she hit. She and Vern are back at the trailer park, but I haven't had a second to myself. She keeps calling to tell me what that Jehovah's Witness is doing. You know she's already gotten her fired from Woolworth's. Do I have to talk to Doris now that Bubba's dead? Doesn't that legally nullify our relationship? I have to find out. What's new with you, anyway? I've taken up backgammon. Vera and I are playing every afternoon; she's not so bad for somebody who chose to live around here of her own will. She lets ghosts come and go like nothing. Bubba drops by once in a while, she says, but she won't let him open her mouth to speak. She thinks he's going to get tired of coming if he can't get a word in, but I told her I wouldn't be so sure. He hooked onto that CB talk—breaker breaker, ten-four good buddy, pedal to the metal—and wouldn't give it up till way after everybody else had stopped using it. He never even had a CB, Maylou, he just did the talk around the house and expected me to know what he was getting at."

"I may have a job," Maylou said, "writing to sell plus-size clothes for women. Zak's off hunting so I haven't come face to face yet. I don't mind him not being here. I'm dreading putting my mama under ground. Summer, at least though, is gentle on earth dwellers, I've been thinking. I'm keeping my chin up," Maylou said. "I'm taking small steps." Things always sounded simpler when you were talking on the phone, Maylou thought. Saying things and doing them were night and day.

"Congrats on the job prospect," CeCe said. "I meant to call you, but with Doris driving me nuts, I've been avoiding the phone. John is on a Greyhound bus probably almost there now. Yesterday he announced a hiatus from his Hopeful Forest. He wants to bury your mama after all, deliver her to the Gates of Heaven himself, then he says he will be back. Those trees are a powerful lodestone to him. Who's to say John's not some latter-day saint, Maylou. Poor Larry got a shiner walking into a tree. He and Bubba are cut from the same cloth, which is natural, I suppose. I'm trying deliberately to stay off Larry's back. Oh," CeCe said, "I just wish you could see how really happy I am, Maylou. If I had my druthers Sher and I would waltz in one another's arms until the cows come home. He is a trophy."

Maylou heard a long intake of air and then a satisfied, and embellished, exhale.

"I'm smoking, Maylou." CeCe blew out again. "Can you tell? Sher says Opal's development won't be affected by it. He says I shouldn't deny myself oral pleasures, isn't that sweet? I hope Opal Jean—OJ, we're going to call her—will love me as much as you loved your mama, Maylou. She must have made a point of skin-to-skin bonding and on-demand breast-feeding, in order to inspire such commitment from you. Your mama probably picked you up the second you cried."

"Zak could've learned a thing or two from her about devotion. I think to win big in love you have to put your chips on one number at a time."

Maylou was doodling Mildred on a notepad, perfect thanks to her pen's plastic surgery. She wrote AFTER underneath the good-looking donkey, BEFORE under a mess with legs. She was thinking maybe the packmule was becoming too big a part of her life.

"Based on your own hearsay, Maylou," CeCe was going on, "Zak's no prize. Don't let him filibuster you into staying with him. You want a man with whom you're equipotent or better. Play the lone ranger where Zak's concerned. He wants to go surfing in the sea of love, you tell him you forgot your board." CeCe sucked in and blew out, relishing, Maylou could tell.

"If my husband was a car," Maylou said, "he'd be well equipped, with mag wheels and a convertible top. I think though, I want fewer options and a roof that stays down. I don't want a car with so much horsepower it's always pulling at the reins. I want a car that will stay parked where I leave it and have a full tank of gas ready to take me where I'm going. Zak's fuel rides on empty most nights though he'd never admit it. He joined Vic Tanny's to prove something but never went and so never did."

Maylou felt mildly guilty telling her husband's secret but from now on her loyalty was to herself. CeCe had become a friend. Maylou thought she was the kind of friend too, blunt enough in her own right, that Maylou could wend not-so-nice stuff into the conversation and get honest feedback on it.

"Next time I talk to you," CeCe said, "I want to hear that Zak is no longer an issue. Back to Sher and I. We've set a nuptial date—the forthcoming autumnal equinox, September 22nd. I want you to be my matron of honor. Vera's already accepted to do it, if you can't. She's sewing my dress from a picture I saw in *Today's Bride*. I'm sending out engraved invitations." CeCe paused to yell at Oscar. "Your stupid dog keeps jumping on my lap. Doesn't he know I hate his pointy face and useless legs. I think he's trying to get to my cigarettes. Let me know as soon as you can about the bridesmaid thing. I thank my lucky stars every time I blink that I've been blessed in love. Sher says we're going to Niagara Falls for our honeymoon."

"Get your picture taken in a barrel then," Maylou said, "it's pretty much de rigueur in that town." She added a bride-like doodle to her other. "I was just thinking, CeCe, sometimes it seems no matter what fits into a conversation, people are going to say what's on their minds at the time anyway. One-sided dialogues are the best most of us can muster. Top priorities vary widely. I wonder about communication. You can say one thing and mean another. Or say nothing and mean something, or something and mean nothing. It's very confusing."

"People like to hear the sound of their own voice, Maylou. I do. Vera's sister Erline, on the other hand, married a man with a gimpy ankle because he hardly said a word. She thought he was mysterious. He put one of those lantern-wielding piccaninny lawn ornaments on the grass in front of their bait store without saying a thing about it. Erline had to end the relationship because her new husband acted without motivation and couldn't converse at meals. His being mysterious was all in her head. She got together his things and piccaninny and sent him packing. Soon after, she missed his quiet company and moved him right back in. Now she says he's her wall of comfort. Erline drives Vera nuts with her topsy-turvy emotions."

"In the love department I think we're mostly all afraid of our feelings," Maylou said, waxing philosophical. "One or two flummoxes is all it takes to provoke a wallflowerish existence. It's feast or famine in love. Zak sure seems small potatoes when I'm hungry."

"Your husband's good parts would fit into a doggie bag, Maylou," CeCe said. "Don't piddle your love away. Keep on rubbernecking until you find Prince Charming is my advice. Like me. Though actually, it wasn't like I had to go looking. Don't tell, Maylou, but I'm going to have another cigarette, which makes me a chain-smoker." Maylou heard CeCe strike a match, draw in and blow out. She wondered if anything got as far as CeCe's lungs with all that windy fanfare.

It was nice to have a girlfriend though, Maylou thought, to talk about things and nothing with. "I'm glad you're sharing your conclusions with me, CeCe," she said. "I guess, love-wise, I don't want to end up by myself. Though really I'm thinking ahead, since I haven't even finished with Zak yet. I'm still married. He's off hunting I can only guess what. I had a shred of hope that maybe he would change while I was away seeing to mama, he told me he had when I spoke to him on the phone. But later, a woman I knew of answered wearing my slinky French slip. First I'm ready to say good-bye to him, then I'm not. I don't know what's the matter with me. I'm somebody whose feet get cold in bed and who likes to sleep like spoons. In those ways I'm romantic."

Maylou wasn't sure there was a man out there with her name on him, let alone some Prince Charming, but she thought she'd take CeCe's advice and have a look. The same way she would peruse all the things on a menu from top to bottom before knowing exactly what it was she wanted to eat. Maylou figured any Mr. Right would seem the spiciest dish around.

CeCe inhaled deeply and let smoke waft in puffs from her nose as she talked, or so it sounded to Maylou from her end. "You should take up smoking, Maylou. Men think it's sexy, if you do it right. You have a lot to offer a man, you know," she went on. "A pretty nape and a perfect driving record not the least of which. Men are willing to settle for far less. Take Vern. Sher and I never tire of whispering love words into each other's ears. We are like kids again, open to life's subtle nuances. You don't have to be a fly on the wall to see our mirth. We live a charmed picnic."

"I'm glad," Maylou said, envious with a grain of salt.

"A cloud is in the foreground of your sky, Maylou, but it will pass," CeCe rolled. "A little bird told me showers bring flowers. Hydrangeas will bloom."

"Thank you, CeCe. I believe in hope," Maylou said. "A life jacket's dangling and I'm swimming for it like sixty."

"You have a winning attitude. I'm not losing any sleep over your woes since before you know it you'll be painting the town red. I better let Oscar out before he makes a mess on the rug again. By the way, Vern said to drop him a line if you wanted to. He talked about your smile. He said when you smile he sees beyond the Pearly Gates into that delightful place where the air is said to be filled with ambrosia. His words, of course." CeCe exhaled, hoping for sexpot-like disdain, Maylou thought. "He exaggerates the way poison ivy itches."

Seventeen

MAYLOU SAT ON THE LOVE SEAT next to Emmanuel
in his van fragrant and brimming with flowers, parked in the
Gates of Heaven cemetery. It was raining cats and dogs. John
had come and gone. Flossie rested gentle under ground, held
to breast in Mother Earth's tireless arms.

Maylou had run into the clairvoyant, Red Dog, at a
Baskin-Robbins ice cream parlor earlier that day. He'd asked
how she was doing since their first meeting, in which he
remembered Maylou contacting her mama but still having
some hard questions after. Before she could speak, he offered
to buy her the ice cream he knew in a flash she wanted, and
then they could sit down and talk.

Red Dog went up to the counter and chose for Maylou.
A girl with a high ponytail, wearing pink on pink, had her
scoop ready to dish out what he wanted. He ordered
Maylou's, and then a bowl of the extra-charge vanilla for
himself. He told the girl to add colored sprinkles, M&Ms.
Oreo bits, and Gummi Bears. "All that and hope too," he
said. "Fill me up with all the toppings in those jars. Be
unscrimpy with your hand, child." As he paid her, their
fingers touched and he said, "Watch out for a boy with the
initials J.D., he'll steal your heart and your daddy's Tercel."

When they were seated, Maylou told Red Dog she felt like a vessel of opportunity and unleashable vigor, but was tired and some shaken. Missing her mama made her stay awake nights, caused her to look at women with graying hair and sensible shoes with a singular desire for affection they hadn't seen in such force elsewhere but in a lover's eyes. She felt like she was in a fog, just trusting her feet to keep taking steps, one after one, until she could break out the other side into clearing. And when she did, Maylou told him, everything should be sun-glowy and fresh, free of sad history, and promise-laden or it wouldn't be worth it all.

"Your feelings are right, and coming in their natural order," Red Dog said. "Eat up, child. To do with the future I would say most of us live in too cluttered a space." Soon after, he left.

Maylou turned to Emmanuel in the van.

"Love is the answer," he was saying. "Take a good look at me, Maylou. I am the man who's going to change your life. I am neither the world's best citizen, nor the worst. I am not detail-oriented, I cannot tell twins apart. I want to bowl you over. I want us to survive on a diet of hope and grapefruits. Grapefruits for their proven overall health benefits. The raw truth is, I love you. A ten-ton truck could not have hit me any harder. Every night I will lay a whisper on your pillow. Every night I will want to hootchy-kootchy, whether we do or not. I will never act the bigshot or call you the little wife or my old bag. I will remain yours truly as long as there is breathable air."

"You make a good case for yourself," Maylou said. "I know Zak will never kick his wandering ways, and all my pretty lingerie will perish to flings, and one-night stands who promise to return what they never will. Besides, I've lost that loving feeling, now it's gone gone gone. My husband is at best an old flame, a near-dead ember." She guessed she'd better snuff it out altogether and stop holding onto a past that wasn't even great.

"Say sayonara, babe. Get it over with," Emmanuel said. "We'll both feel better." He pushed a music tape into the cassette player and pressed rewind. "Divorce is no longer a badge of shame. Let's go where the sun always shines and there's never a dull moment, where humdrum is outlawed and fancy free is king." He pressed play. "Let's go where Memphis Minnie sings the best train blues we've ever heard, non-stop."

"She sings with pure exasperation," Maylou said, feeling lighter, going with the flow of the music. "I can hear the chuga-chug of the Chickasaw train picking up men all down the line. I see those lowdown, dirty dogs loving and leaving her. I like the way old Minnie picks a guitar."

"Maylou," Emmanuel said, "hear Peetie Wheatstraw the Devil's Son-in-Law on piano. Cripple Clarence Lofton on drums, Mezz Mezzrow on bass. Fly with me. Take a magic-carpet ride straight to the chapel of love." Emmanuel clasped her hands in his and closed his eyes. He felt the blues spouting on and off like a faucet.

Maylou kissed his sun-browned hands. She held them back away from her to look. It was then that she saw the thorn. A dark rose shadow under the surface of the skin on his finger. Emmanuel's eyes were closed and his lips were moving to the shape of the words being sung. Had he thought about it, he would have believed Maylou was kissing his finger. She got the lay of the thorn with her tongue, then sank her bottom teeth in underneath it. She fitted the thorn between her upper and lower teeth and pulled her head back as hard as she could. She pulled the thorn still tucked in skin, from her mouth, smiling from ear to ear.

"No pain, no gain," she said. "I used to go through life like a breeze. But the moment that thorn came unstuck from your finger, I felt love burn in me like a fever. I felt the uprighteous certainty of a split-second decision years in the making. Emmanuel, you are the it I want to put my heart and soul into. You are my wherefore and why."

Emmanuel kissed Maylou's hair, her neck, her eyelids. He promised not only himself, but lilac-scented dreams, nights of everlasting love, passion to move mountains. Maylou blinked back tears. She saw, in the dim light of the van, Emmanuel swaying over her, vast and blurred, the way a mother must look to her newly delivered child.

Maylou was about to put an end to her marriage. As she drove her car around the corner of her street, she saw Lowanda carrying an end table and a ginger-jar bedside lamp. Lowanda was making her way clumsily across her drive and up to the open front door of her house. Maylou waved but Lowanda only hurried her pace, her eyes jumpy and proprietary. Once through the door, Lowanda did wave back, but briefly, before slamming the door closed behind her. The end table, the bedside lamp, Maylou's personal possessions no longer.

It was then Maylou saw the small crowd of people gathered on her front lawn. She saw Zak hammering a "Yard Sale—Bargains Bargains" sign into the damp grass near the sidewalk. Neighbors and others were picking through her things, opening and closing cupboard doors, turning tables over to check for neat joins underneath. Her chest of drawers, bed frame, rocking chair, dishes, toiletries, books, shoes, clothes, everything was laid out on the lawn. Maylou's heart squeezed into her throat. Zak had dealt a low blow.

Grace Hinkle, ninety if a day, was flexing her feet in Maylou's Nike hightops. Maylou parked her car in the drive. Grace Hinkle bounded over.

"The tag says ten dollars but that can't be right for a pair of sneakers," the old lady said, looking down at her feet. "And they're used. I'll give you five. I've got to make my old-age pension money stretch. I've got to buy food and a doll for Lindsey's birthday and aspirin to thin my blood. I shouldn't be browsing at all. I should be knitting a little doll and not worrying about my blood. If it wants to clot up I should go ahead and let it. I should let this old body kick the bucket if that's what it wants to do. I'm tired of being thrifty and counting my pennies. You get what you pay for. It's better to invest in a few quality things that will last, than to throw your money down the toilet on cheap crap. I'll give you two-fifty for these ankle grazers, take it or leave it." Grace Hinkle stood firm.

"I wouldn't dream of usurping your pension," Maylou said, charitably, under the circumstances. "Go ahead and run with those shoes. Today you were a smart shopper who bagged a bargain. Today you are the cat's meow."

Grace Hinkle eyed her. "Something is never gotten for nothing," she said. "Somewhere down the line I'll pay through the nose for this windfall. I can only hope I won't live long enough to be caught up with. I hope these running shoes run me straight to the Kingdom of Heaven. Till then I want to feel like a girl again. Then I could walk for miles and never have an ache in my sole, my head so stuck up in the clouds my feet never scraped dirt. I was airy as a feather, the center of my optimistic universe."

"Those shoes'll get you where you're going in a jiffy," Maylou said. "They look like they were made for you."

"Watch my dust," Grace Hinkle said on departure.

Zak was raking in money, his pants drooped with it. Maylou saw two nosey parkers cooing over her heirloom vanity. Zak hadn't emptied her belongings from it, and they were onto her and her predicament.

Maylou sauntered towards them having some pride remaining. "Many a night I have been dynamically wooed," she said. "Even my toenails incited rapture and mirthful bouts of licking. This stomped love wasn't always that. What you're seeing here is something naughty and sad. Look away, look away. My marriage is sour grapes."

"The human heart is a brave but stupid organ," one of the women said. "Always expect the worst. It's best to live like you feel reckless and pretty. Put yourself first in all things. A good night's sleep with babylike dreams will go a long way. Slop and betrayal are part and parcel of the human condition. These are things I've come to know."

"My spirit is not so bogged with dread as you'd think," Maylou said. "I feel plucky. My spouse beat me to the punch, is all. My whole kit and caboodle spread out on the lawn was a surprise. I've found another man I think is supreme and with whom I want to spend my nights in an athletic tangle. I've landed a good job. Mostly I'm on the upswing." The words themselves made her feel better. She'd talk tough, and keep on talking tough, until her heart knew the words and raced on beyond.

"Far be it from us to be naysayers, sweet bird of youth," the cronies said. "Fly, fly, fly. Flap, flap, flap."

Maylou watched her things being portaged away by neighbors and strangers alike. She felt mild relief. Freed of possessions, she would be lighter, quicker on the draw, ready to jump at a moment's notice. She'd rightly place value on her own knowable center. Personal trappings were just that. Her best bet in hard times was herself.

Zak was talking to a group of his friends who had gathered around.

"Boys," he was saying, "love is not a toy. Commitment is a nice thing for many. When I'm with a hot tamale I feel like a daredevil and that feeling is hard to beat. It makes me feel grand. I see my wife is home early, which blows a hole in my plan to almost vanish. Maybe I'm a fool, boys. Either way, the next phase of my life is about to begin. Let the words hard-bitten and sparky come to mind when you think of me. Remember me as a nomad. A lover of women for their curves."

Maylou took her wedlocked man aside. "I'm kissing you and my possessions off," she said. "I'm an emporium of hurt feelings. What were you hoping to accomplish with this petty mongering?"

Maylou really did have only her own self now. Used to be she'd look at her things, her brass bed, her teapots, and see her character reflected in them. Like her clothes, they were outward displays of who she was, her personal style, and the sight of them always reinforced the way she saw herself. Now she'd have to sit naked on a bare floor and get familiar with her inner tickings. Cloak herself in good-feeling futures with silky outcomes.

"Leaving was uppermost on your mind," Zak said. "I've been inhaling good riddance for weeks, just waiting for the axe to fall. You loved me once, you love me no more. Philandering is something I'm not keen to lay aside. Folly is not behind me. I needed some money practically, and a clean slate emotionally, before skipping our lackluster marriage. A yard sale looked like the ticket." Zak jangled coins in his pocket.

"I want a one-woman man I can stand by and show the world I love," Maylou said. "You are not that man. I'm for new beginnings and honest relations. It wouldn't be fair for you to keep the profits from the sale of my stuff. Now that we've come to our final curtain, you won't catch me being taken for a ride."

"Shoot," Zak said.

"I have seen heartache and licked it," Maylou said gaining on him. "A lot of water's gone under my bridge. Despair knows my first name. I have put up and shut up, for what? As a husband you were all thumbs, bub."

"I was hoping I might jag your memory as something hard and warm you once knew. Somebody you curled around like a spoon late at night. Maybe my image of myself is inflated. This tearless split should bring me down a notch or two. I hope it will cut me down to a more manageable size for the next dalliance down the road."

Zak emptied his pockets into Maylou's waiting hands.

"Now I'm empty-handed," he said. "That's how I'm going away. It's what a crud like me deserves. I'd like to say, keep a place for me in your heart, but I see already there's no room. In another life maybe things will be different for us. Maybe I'll be born a co-worker and you can take me for what I am, without suffering nights of jealous worry." Zak looked around the yard. "Purely from a business standpoint, this was a good idea," he said. "Now you can treat yourself to something special. I guess you'll have to."

"Things will be shipshape in no time," Maylou said, hoping to self-fulfil a prophecy. "Soon even my innermost thoughts will be splendid. I won't be hoodwinked or snowed. All my interiors will shine like King Tut's tomb."

"Don't give me a second thought," Zak said. "I think I have Sybil-like tendencies for now I feel kind of sorry."

"Be frolicsome and pert," Maylou said. "But be it somewhere else."

That night in her near-empty house, Maylou looked at the doodads nobody wanted and thought, the world is a crooked place. Whoever it was pulling her strings had made his point. She was a lone puppet on a bare stage. She longed for fragrant thoughts. Recognize the good in things, she told herself, stamp out misery. Be pleasant and forthright. Do unto others and tie up loose ends. The phone rang.

"Like in a vision I thought I should call," John said. "I pictured the sprinklers whirling and looping over your mama's grave. You standing in a light mist. I miss her like you would miss anything beautiful. I always considered your mama to be within an eyelash of dazzling though I never told her so, I was known as the silent type. Are you all right?"

"I was just taking inventory on that. Seems I only get to some insight after tramping through bramble and thicket. I sneak in the back door of understanding, my feet cut and sore from the overgrown path I had to walk to get there. Zak has been a disappointment to my heart, which I've known for a while he would be. I have a new man though. I'm responding well to his honeyed words. He tells me he's no pink elephant and I believe him."

"For some, love is an acquired taste," John said. "I was lucky to have enjoyed your mama and her spicy cooking for so long."

"Mama's love was like an umbrella. Without it of late, I've been soaked to the skin." That wasn't the half of it though, Maylou thought. She felt like she'd seen something terrible and couldn't erase the vision from her mind. The imprint of it had changed the way she saw things, like her eyes now saw sadness, traces of it everywhere she turned.

"Maylou, your mama found winds refreshing, rainstorms soothing. She wouldn't have minded you getting wet. Be brave to the elements and let the sun shine in when it will. Your mama was the best medicine I ever had and she would have thrown herself in front of a train for you. It's natural we're both woozy and sentimental."

"I yen for some last word," Maylou said. "I feel like I got cut off. I want to tell her what I've learned, how I plan to live my life. I think mama would want to know the kind of person I'm going to become. I don't think she'd feel comfortably settled until she saw the results of her maternal upbringing. I have to first know exactly what it is I've learned, and then I have to put it just rights."

"Words can be as hard as sprites to pin down," John said. "And fairies can kiss their own elbows, which is how baffling they are."

Emmanuel entered Topeka's Gates of Heaven in the morning's magic hour with the light soft and warm, tolerant of newly awakened eyes. He did what he usually did in the morning, which was to wander the deserted cemetery, whistling through the graveyard, checking out the flowers on the headstones. He could then stock up on what was popular, and keep in his van a constant display of the tried and true. He drank a take-out coffee in a styrofoam cup as he went. He liked being the only man walking upright, monolithic. Mornings, Emmanuel felt at the peak of his powers.

The cemetery sprinklers were whirling and looping over the graves, setting a fine mist of water glistening on everything. Morning has broken, Emmanuel thought, sunlight from God's own skies. Lying her knees curled up, her head tucked into her chest, across her mama's grave, was the object of his affection.

"Maylou," he said. "Wake and espy the clear heavens. The world is sprawling and nearly perfect. It's a gladsome sight. Desperadoes even would find cheer in it. It's me, Emmanuel."

Maylou opened her eyes and saw his turquoise ones looking back simpatico.

"You're wet from the sprinklers," he said, and put his arm around her. He gave her his hot cup of coffee to hold between her hands. "Are you mine, babe?" he said. "Are we done with mopery and tribulation?"

"Zak's gone," Maylou said. "What's left for us is the lofty-most half of love, plus gleeful times. Blight has scooted."

Maylou stood and stretched out her arms, reaching skyward. "Last night I came to this place and whipped like a dervish. The constellations were shining overhead, the seven sparkling stars of the Big Dipper, the ever-bright Dog Star, the fishy scales of Pisces, opaline. I wanted to find my way clear of the inert weight of the past, quell the mumbo jumbo in my head. I wanted to cha-cha or something unto-ward. I thought maybe my mama might notice me whirling and come."

"And did she?" Emmanuel said.

"No. But under the stars and the silvery light of the moon it came to me," Maylou said. "I bloomed like a night flower. My petals unfolded to the stinging winds of truth, my roots drew from the earth the sweet nectar of life. For an instant, I shimmered with care and want. I heard my heart in my ears. All things give up their breath, I heard. Hope springs internal. Go willingly, and twinklingly, to the end of a thing. That is all there is to know."

Maylou regarded her manly heartthrob. "It was a big relief," she said. "I can tell you."